A LAMENTATION
OF SWANS

By the Author

Slash and Burn

A Lamentation of Swans

A LAMENTATION
OF SWANS

by

Valerie Bronwen

2017

A LAMENTATION OF SWANS

ISBN 13: 978-1-62639-828-3

THIS TRADE PAPERBACK ORIGINAL IS PUBLISHED BY
BOLD STROKES BOOKS, INC.
P.O. BOX 249
VALLEY FALLS, NY 12185

FIRST EDITION: AUGUST 2017

CREDITS
EDITOR: RUTH STERNGLANTZ
PRODUCTION DESIGN: STACIA SEAMAN
COVER DESIGN BY MELODY POND

This is for LAUREN,
who shares my love of Mary Stewart and Victoria Holt

CHAPTER ONE

Today I finally faced my past, in order that I might have a future.

A little less than two years ago, I gave up on my marriage and the life I thought my wife and I were building together. I walked out of the home I'd shared with her for just under a year after impetuously getting married and went back to the career I'd foolishly, romantically, given up for my now failed marriage. I was determined to pick up the pieces of my wrecked life, prove to myself and the world that I was somebody, that I did have worth, and somehow rebuild what was left of my self-esteem.

I went back to New York and convinced my old boss to give me my old job back, dedicating myself solely to building my career. I gave up on life and love and friendship, *anything* personal that wouldn't advance my career in some way. It was my work that saved my life and my sanity, just as it had before. I channeled all my energy, all my pain, and the unbearable loneliness that passed for my life into my work.

It paid off, too. That single-minded focus helped me become, at twenty-five, the youngest junior partner in the history of Hollis Allman Interior Designs, and now, after my second year back with the firm, I was in line for a full partnership.

Work was everything to me. It never betrayed me, never made me feel lesser, never made me feel like somehow I wasn't a woman. My days were swatches and blueprints and furniture, lighting and curtains and decorative art. I haunted art galleries looking for up-and-coming artists to sell to my clients. I could walk into an empty house or office or apartment and within a few questions could come up with a design that was so perfect for my clients they couldn't live without it, and I could even convince them it was their idea, not mine. Difficult sell? Management always sent me. A client who was an enormous commission who couldn't make up their mind? Send Ariel in, and a decision would be made. I could manage contractors, herd deliverymen, and coax the most stubborn painting crew into getting back on time.

Losing myself in work was the easiest way I could think of to keep my sanity. I couldn't think about how I'd ruined my marriage by overreacting to everything—by turning the smallest criticism into a fight, by resenting my wife's job and my own loneliness, every one of the enormous and stupid mistakes I'd made—if my mind was always on my work, if I was so exhausted by the time I got back to my apartment with a take-out meal to gobble down before taking something to help me sleep, then I didn't have the energy to look back, to reflect on my own stupidity and naïveté and childishness, and what I could have done better, how I could have been a better wife, how I could have saved my marriage instead of wrecking it.

How every time I came to a fork in the road I, without fail, chose the wrong path.

But I kept telling myself, on those rare moments when I curled up with my cat and a bottle of wine, alone in my apartment on yet another Saturday night in the most exciting city in the world, with no friends to call, no dates, no nothing but emptiness, that dwelling on mistakes wouldn't change anything, and went on convincing myself that everything was all in the past and the best thing for me to do was to keep moving ahead, getting on with my life, becoming one of the top interior designers in New York City, and thus the world.

But what kind of life was it, really? Up at six every morning and in the office by eight, sometimes not getting home until almost ten. I carved out time every week to meet a trainer at the gym, to keep my body fit—those lonely Saturday nights with wine and ice cream and Netflix were dangerous to my waist and my hips—and sometimes I went for spa days, getting massages and mani-pedis and facials. I shopped at expensive stores and had my hair cut and shampooed and styled and colored at the best salons. It was all, as my boss Hollis always reminded me, a part of the package I was selling to our clients.

"The rich, the kind of people we want as clients," Hollis said, glancing at me approvingly after my first appointment with her stylist, "want to hire people who understand their wants, what they need. No one wants to hire a decorator with no style, who looks like her last job was waiting tables at Hooters." She smiled. "Every cent you spend on how you look will come back a hundredfold from clients. You have to look *expensive*."

She laughed, running one perfectly manicured hand through her perfectly coiffed short red hair, which fell immediately back into place. "But you don't have to spend a lot of money. Watch for sales—especially sample sales. There are websites that sell designer stuff for next to nothing—shoes, bags, clothes—I'll have my assistant text you the links." Her gray eyes flashed behind her fashionable red-framed glasses. She gestured at the dove-gray Chanel suit she was wearing, the matching Jimmy Choos on her feet. "I didn't spend more than two hundred dollars on this entire ensemble." She looked at me over the top of her glasses, which always slid down to the tip of her slightly upturned nose. The Jimmy Choos added a couple of inches to her height, but she was still barely five-three. Workouts with a trainer kept her slim figure ridiculously tiny. "And trust me—don't skimp on your underwear, either. Even if no one sees it." She held up a hand to stop me from answering. "No, I don't care about your personal life. What you do on your own time isn't my concern. But when you wear nice things…it gives you confidence. And that confidence helps get clients."

She was right, as she so often was.

I had to look like I had my shit together, and so I did—at least when I was at work.

I was always available to my clients and my boss, 24/7. That accessibility and drive made me invaluable to my boss, and that's why there was absolutely no doubt I would make full partner within another year.

And on those occasional Saturday nights when I gave in to the memories and let them out, after watching some romantic movie and drinking too much wine, even at my most hopeful, I never thought I would ever return to Sea Oats.

And I wouldn't have, either, had it not been for the cryptic email Peggy Glaven had sent me several days earlier.

I was checking my email on the subway home, taking a rare early evening because I'd finished with three big projects. I was feeling a bit burned out, and Hollis told me to go home and drink some wine.

"You should take some time off," she advised, pushing her red-framed glasses up her long nose. "You haven't had a vacation since you came back. Someone else can bid these jobs. I don't want you flaming out on me. Take two weeks. Go sit on a beach somewhere."

"But I don't want—"

"Go." She waved me out of her office. The subject was closed. I was on vacation for two weeks.

The last thing I wanted was some time away, with nothing to keep me from remembering, from reliving that year at Sea Oats, going over every excruciating and painful moment where I went wrong, how I lost the only person I'd ever loved.

Would ever love.

I sank down onto my seat on the subway uptown and, like everyone else, pulled out my phone.

And there it was, right in my inbox. The subject line read *Ariel Important Please Read*, and the return email was peggy.glaven@seaoats.com.

Peggy.

I closed my eyes and listened to the rattling of the subway as it hurtled uptown. *Delete it unread, don't pull off the scab, why do you want to do this to yourself.*

I opened my eyes and touched the email.

Ariel,

> *I've missed you so much since you went away. I saw the piece in the Sunday* Times *about you, so I know you're doing well. We're all so proud of you. Things here at Sea Oats—well, things aren't good. I do wish you'd come. Will you at least come out for a visit? I'm sure things aren't nearly as bad as you think they are, even after two years. And we need you here. The family needs to come together now more than ever.*

> *Please come.*

> *Love,*
> *Peggy*

It was, I told myself, almost like the universe was giving me a sign.

You need closure, Ariel.

And that was why I found myself on that tourist van driving through the vast gates of Sea Oats, returning after two years, as a visitor rather than as someone who belonged.

Little ever changed at Sea Oats. A fresh coat of paint every so often, the addition of electricity, and repairs of course necessitated slight changes to the original structure, but it was pretty much the same today as it was the day it was built. My keys probably still worked and the remote control for the gate I'd hidden away in the all-purpose drawer in my apartment kitchen undoubtedly would work, if fresh batteries were loaded into it.

But I didn't want to come through the gate, not after all this time. I didn't feel like I had the right to use the keys, although on paper I was still married into the family who'd built Sea Oats and to whom it has always belonged. I also knew that it was cowardly to sneak into the grounds the way I was doing, coming as a tourist during the open hours. But I knew if I paid my twenty dollars I couldn't be turned away, and I also wanted to face my memories on my own terms without being observed, to see if I had the inner strength necessary to face down the Swanns and the past.

It was almost exactly two years ago to the day that I'd packed up my things and fled, humiliated and angry and embarrassed and defeated, wiping away emotional tears. Happily ever after, apparently, lasted less than a year. I thought she would come after me, of course, fool that I was. I was making a dramatic gesture, running away from a fight, running away from cruel words said in the heat of anger. *If she loves me she'll come after me*, I thought on the train back into the city, suitcases shoved on the rack above my seat, staring out the window. *And I know she loves me.*

But she didn't come.

She just let me go.

I couldn't believe it.

She'd never loved me.

But that naïve and foolish girl was gone now. I might have buried myself in work and avoided getting close to anyone since I'd left, but my wounds had toughened into scars. My hide was thicker and my tongue sharper, and I'd become more of a fighter.

And I'd learned that frequently negotiation is an easier way to get what you want than fighting.

I wasn't that stupid wide-eyed girl who'd come here as a bride with her eyes and heart wide open, madly in love and easily hurt.

And still…I wasn't any more sure now than I was then what waited for me at Sea Oats, but at least I was better prepared.

Or so I thought.

Everything seemed the same, like it was only yesterday that I'd walked out on my marriage. There's a timeless quality about Sea Oats that nothing can quite shake. Sea Oats still belongs to another period, when servants were cheap and the wealthy spared no expense in building their homes—homes that were symbols of their wealth and power. Home to the Swann family, built just after the Civil War with money earned from California gold mines and railroads in the Midwest and shipping and, of course, Swann's. Now it was an enormous old white elephant that cost a fortune to maintain, to heat, to clean. The house was still beautiful, though, a Victorian mansion with clean lines and towers and porches and balconies and ornate railings. It was originally intended to be one of two summer homes so the family could escape the heat and grime of Manhattan in the summertime—the other being the cottage in Newport. But most of New York society summered in Newport, so Sea Oats, on the Atlantic side of Long Island, was for peace and quiet and escape. The mansion on Fifth Avenue was long gone, sold and turned into a chain hotel before the Second World War. The place in Newport was now a museum, owned and operated by the state.

The Swanns have only Sea Oats left, and since I left they've started opening it daily in the afternoons for tours of one hour at twenty dollars a head, with coffee and pastries concluding the tour in the kitchen. I'd been stunned, when I checked into the picturesque inn in the village of Penobscot, to see the tour brochure on the desk in my room. Impulsively I'd decided to take the next one, not bothering to unpack, and dashed across the street to the little tourist information storefront. I hadn't recognized the woman working there, nor did I know our tour guide, which was kind of a relief. I hadn't spent much time in Penobscot itself when I lived at Sea Oats, and I'm not sure what I would have done had either of the women recognized me.

The sight of the towering oaks lining the driveway, the vast expanse of green lawn, the fountains bubbling in the sunshine sent a slight chill down my spine. I was here, back where I thought—had *sworn*—I would never return. My stomach fluttered and I felt a wave of nausea from nerves. It wasn't too late. I could slip into the house, hide with the tour, and slip right back out again with no one the wiser. I was wearing a rain slicker, with a large hood that fell over my forehead and hid my face in shadows. With the hood up, no one would get a clear look at my face.

I steeled myself and pushed those thoughts away.

It had been almost two years. I had made it this far. I wasn't going to turn back now. I didn't know what my plan was—I hadn't thought that far ahead. Just coming out here, renting a room in town...I hadn't really thought beyond that. The tour had been a godsend, seemed like a gift too good to pass up. I didn't have to do anything. I could just take the tour, get a feel for the place, see what emotions and memories it dredged up, curl up in my room back at the inn with a bottle of wine, and figure out what to do then.

Maybe I would just get back on a train in the morning and go back into the city.

I've learned that it's always best to have options.

There were clouds out to sea, and there was a slight chill to the early spring air. Rain was on its way, which gave me the excuse I needed to keep the hood of my jacket up, even though the interior of the tour van was overheated.

No one had to know I'd come back until and unless I wanted them to know.

There, just beyond the side of the house, was the big pond. And the hedge maze, that damned hedge maze. That was part of the tour, of course, a trip into the famous hedge maze of Sea Oats. That was what everyone on the tour wanted to see, at least from what I'd gathered listening to them talk while we waited to board the van. They didn't care about the house, or the grounds. The maze had been in *Architectural Digest* and *Better Homes & Gardens* and had been featured, more than once, in every major newspaper's Sunday issues. One of the selling points of the tour I'd paid for was it included a chance to go inside the maze—*Everyone Gets a Chance to Walk the Famous Maze!!!*

People wandering onto the grounds to see it had always been an issue—maybe the tours were a way of keeping trespassers off the grounds, rather than a required income stream. There were twenty of us on the tour van, that was four hundred dollars. Five tours a day, Monday through Saturday, would be a nice chunk of change—if every tour was sold out.

I hadn't heard that Swann's was in trouble, but I didn't pay attention to business news.

And as for that damned hedge maze, I could go the rest of my life without ever seeing it again. I'd always hated it.

I planned on ducking out of the tour before then.

The van swung out to the right, following the tree-lined drive as it expanded out into a circle.

The sunlight glinted on the surface of the pond, but its depths were as dark and mysterious as ever.

There were no swans there, of course, and I found myself blinking back unexpected tears.

Get a hold of yourself or you're not going to make it, I reminded myself. I got my emotions under control as the van pulled up in front of the big Victorian house.

A swan would have been too much to hope for.

I heard her voice saying, *You know there's a legend about the pond...that a swan will appear there whenever a Swann has found true love.*

The problem with legends was people believed in them sometimes.

Our tour guide was one of those saccharinely happy women who thought orders given with a smile and a pleasant tone like that of a kindergarten teacher would disguise that she meant to be obeyed. I'd tuned out her incessant patter, which began as soon as everyone was safely inside the van and it had pulled away from the curb in front of the tourist information center in the historic village of Penobscot, Long Island. She wouldn't be easy to get away from—I could tell she was one of those ruthlessly efficient women who'd do periodic head counts and had guaranteed Peggy that no tourist would ever be left behind when the van had left the premises. She had the local accent, though, and I was a little surprised her face didn't look familiar to me. I might not have mixed much with the neighbors during my year at Sea Oats, but it surprised me she wasn't one of the local women who'd occasionally come out to visit, with invitations to join clubs and other things I wasn't interested in.

Where did you come from, Karen? I wondered as the house came into view from my window and I caught my breath.

Sea Oats was an enormous house, even for its time, when the summer cottages of the wealthy in Newport were larger than many modern hotels. The architect, Arthur Van Wyck, had done many houses up in the Hudson Valley and had also designed some of the Newport cottages. It was constructed entirely of wood, which meant many repairs over the years, due to storm damage and wood rot. It looked like it had been painted since my unceremonious departure, a fresh coat of dark green paint on the main structure and the trim done in bright yellow—green and yellow had been Arabella Swann's favorite colors, and the house had been built for her by an older, doting husband who'd never been able to deny her anything she wanted.

I'd always been slightly intimidated by the place. The first time I'd seen it, when I'd been invited out for a weekend to meet and get to know the rest of the family, I'd been taken aback. I'd known Charlotte Swann was a wealthy woman who lived on an estate on the Atlantic shore of Long Island, but seeing pictures of Sea Oats online didn't prepare me at all for the reality.

"All right, here we are!" Karen our tour guide announced brightly as the driver pulled up in front of the stairs up to the veranda and put the van into neutral. There was a hydraulic hiss as the doors opened. "Remember to stay with the group and that the upper floors are off-limits!"

Dutifully we all climbed out of the van, like obedient children. She counted as we each passed her, going down the two steps and stepping out onto the pavement.

I moved aside so those behind me could climb down and stared up at the house.

It was just a house. Looking at it now, I couldn't believe I'd been so intimidated by it.

I'd been so young and stupid.

Around the side of the house the pond lay, brooding.

I hung back behind the rest of the twenty tour participants, an odd mixture of tourists from the Midwest and foreigners— I'd heard several of them speaking to each other in French— mostly couples, some small children, a couple of teenagers with their eyes glued to their phones. I wondered if I could manage to slip away when everyone else went inside. Karen the tour guide had the eyes of an eagle—she seemed like the kind of organized person who carefully made lists and crossed them off, probably covered her living room furniture in plastic. I shook my head. That wasn't fair. I couldn't blame her for being so attentive. The responsibility to avoid the potential liability of someone getting away from her group on the Swann estate was more than enough to put the fear of God in her, I'm sure—and so I allowed her to herd me up the front steps, across the wide, solid porch, and inside the stained-glass front door with its *Swan Lake* imagery.

The enormous foyer was exactly as I remembered it. Nostalgia almost overwhelmed me as I again stood in the big round room with the heavily varnished mahogany floor, the enormous sparkling chandelier overhead, the mirrors and the door to the coatroom, the marvelous hanging staircase to the second floor. It was warm inside, but Karen made no offer to take our coats. Some of the others in the group did remove theirs, draping them over their arms, but not only did I keep mine on, I left the hood up. Karen did give me an odd look when she shepherded us into the big drawing room to the left of the foyer and I came face-to-face with the famous old painting of the old robber baron himself, over the fireplace.

The painting was the only part of the room I'd ever been able to stand. When the house was built, the room was intended for men only, to withdraw to after dinner for brandy and cigars so they could talk about manly topics that were too much for their featherbrained women to wrap their little minds around. The room was a monument to nineteenth-century sexism and masculinity: the patriarchy displayed as a room. The dark-paneled walls were festooned with a variety of animal heads, their glassy eyes staring vacantly out, trophies of barbaric slaughter from a different time when such things were held in higher esteem. The long dead animals had always given me the creeps. I'd always wanted to redecorate the room, get rid of the grisly heads, and make it more warm and inviting than it was with its heavy, dark wooden furniture that just screamed virility and male privilege.

You could almost smell the stale cigar smoke, hear the brandy being poured into snifters.

That was just one of the many battles I'd lost during the year I'd lived here. I'd always thought of it as Samuel's room, and it was dominated by his full-length portrait. He glared out from narrowed eyes with his lips curled in a bit of a sneer, the marquee of the original Swann's Department Store on Amsterdam in Manhattan behind him, a pocket watch in his left hand. Samuel Swann had been a robber baron, made his immense fortune in gold mines and railroads, but his father had been a shopkeeper. Late in his life, Samuel opened Swann's.

The family legend held that he opened the store to honor the memory of his father, but Swann's made his fortune even vaster than he could have ever dreamed, taking him up to the same level as the Vanderbilts and the Rockefellers, creating an empire that still exists today.

Swann's wasn't what it once was, of course. But the chain of stores had survived the upheavals in the market and the changes in how consumers shopped, still going strong.

But there was a twinkle in his eyes—you had to look to see it, but it was there. It softened the grim countenance, and I always liked to think Arabella, his second wife, was the reason it was there.

The furnishings in the drawing room were, of course, priceless antiques. The pieces on the mantel below the painting were Egyptian antiquities. Samuel Swann had made his fortune during the time when wealthy Americans were looting the world of whatever treasure they could pay for and illicitly cart away. His second wife, young Arabella, also fancied herself a patroness of the arts. Samuel could deny Arabella nothing, or so the stories say, and so he allowed her to turn all three of his homes into museums. Most of the original collection was now in actual museums, of course, but there were plenty of gorgeous and valuable pieces still in the Sea Oats collection. I noted that some side tables and chairs weren't the same ones I remembered being there. Peggy had probably moved the more fragile, valuable pieces upstairs and away from strangers' eyes and the dangers posed by Starbucks coffee cups and Big Gulps and children's sticky fingers.

I managed to get away from the group sooner than I'd expected or hoped.

I walked over to the double doors leading out to the veranda, and while Karen the cheerful tour guide was explaining about

Samuel's safaris in darkest Africa, I managed to unlatch the doors and escape.

I breathed out a sigh of relief and walked along the veranda around to the back steps. My heart was pounding and I felt almost like I was having an out-of-body experience. Being back at Sea Oats after so long...I ran my hand along the varnished railing. Nothing important had changed, from the smells of polish and varnish to the slightly dusty smell inside that no amount of work by cleaners could quite eradicate, to the undoubtedly priceless knickknacks exactly where they were the night I took my exit in a moment of what had been, to me at the time, the highest drama.

Now, older and wiser and slightly more cynical, I knew it had been more like idiocy, French farce, melodrama straight from the script of *The Young and the Restless*. In a moment of youthful bravado and pride and fury, I'd thrown away my marriage, my life, everything that mattered most to me.

Of course, I'd expected Char to come after me. I would have never left had I believed for a minute she would just let me go.

Two years later, I was still waiting.

But...it didn't hurt anymore to think about it. I'd buried the pain deep, certainly, but I could be here without it hurting. I'd walked through the front door without collapsing, and the roof hadn't caved in, either.

The truth was I'd been too young to get married, not emotionally mature enough at twenty-three, no matter what I believed, to handle being a wife and a partner, particularly to a woman like Charlotte Swann.

I walked down the stairs and along the paved path. Sea Oats was an enormous estate, acres and acres of land ending at the Atlantic Ocean at its own private beach. In those honeymoon days when I first came here, I'd taken walks along the beach in the morning after my coffee and sometimes at night before I went to bed, watching the lights on faraway boats out at sea and wondering where they were going. Before my immaturity began to undermine the foundation of our marriage, before my insecurities gained the upper hand in my mind.

I'd been happy here once. I could have been happy here again.

But now it was too late.

I don't know why I'd bothered to come, if I was being completely honest with myself. Peggy's email had just been an excuse. Maybe it was just curiosity? A chance to see the place once more, to see if in the two years since I'd gone that the wounds had healed and scarred over, so I could look at the place dispassionately and not feel the hurt, the longing? I'd told myself many times that I was over Char, that my marriage was over, and I should just hire a lawyer and get it over with once and for all. But I'd never been able to bring myself to do it, had I? I'd gone so far as to look up divorce lawyers who were lesbian friendly several times, but never could quite bring myself to call any of them.

And I could never get the thought out of the back of my mind that Char hadn't initiated a divorce, either.

And when I'd had too much wine and was curled up on the couch in my apartment with my cat, I couldn't help but think the reason she hadn't was because she, too, held out hope that maybe…just maybe…

Hope springs eternal, doesn't it?

I walked past the entrance to the enormous hedge maze. I'd never liked the maze. The symmetry of it, its impenetrability, the things that made it so interesting and a tourist attraction were the very reasons I didn't like it. I'd walked it once when I'd first come and had panicked. With the sun hidden by the eight-foot-high shrubbery and the endless turns and dead ends, it was easy to believe I might not ever find my way out again, my panic growing as I kept making wrong turns and coming to dead ends, terror that I was trapped inside forever growing until I'd finally started screaming. Old Angus, the head groundskeeper, had to come rescue me.

The maze covered an entire acre of the grounds, and Angus was obsessed with it. The story was, of course, that good ole Samuel had taken Arabella on an extended honeymoon in Europe and the Middle East (so many of the Swann treasures came from that trip, when ole Sammy couldn't deny his young bride anything), and she happened to be taken with a hedge maze on an English estate—which one being lost to the mists of time—so she had to have one at Sea Oats. And so he'd created one to make her laugh and smile and clap delightedly.

I hated the thing even more after I'd been lost inside, and refused to ever venture back in. If it had been up to me, it would have been dug up by the roots and sod put down in its place so no one would ever know it had ever existed. I'd had horrible nightmares about the hedge maze, understandably, but I also knew it wasn't going anywhere. It was too much of a showpiece, and Sea Oats was too well known because of it. I knew it wasn't dangerous, and I knew it was just a hedge. But my hatred of it was irrational, and I always hurried past it.

Just beyond was Poseidon's Fountain, one of my favorite places on the grounds. I'd spent a lot of time there during my year at Sea Oats, perched on the edge as water burbled into the basin of the fountain covered in mosaic tiles in multiple shades of blue that supposedly mirrored the Aegean Sea. A large marble trident-clutching statue that had once graced a Grecian temple rose above the splashing waters. I'd often sat there, reading a book, my back turned to the hideous maze, the sound of the water soothing to me just as the waves at the beach were. I smiled as I walked past the just blooming flower beds of early spring and sat on the side of the fountain. Coins glinted in the sun along the blue-tiled bottom of the fountain—that was new, and I couldn't imagine the tourists tossing coins into the water and making wishes pleased Char very much.

Then again, nothing about opening the house to tours would please Char much, unless she'd changed and mellowed since I'd last seen her.

"What a little coward you are, Ariel," I said out loud as I pulled my hood back and allowed my blond hair to fall free. I'd pinned it up before leaving the inn, but since no one seemed to recognize me, letting it down didn't seem quite so risky.

It was almost like I'd never lived here.

That was when I heard the voices, talking angrily.

I panicked a bit. They couldn't see me because I was hidden from them by the maze, but they'd come around the corner soon enough and there was no place for me to hide.

"I don't like it one bit, Peggy." I'd know that voice anywhere, particularly when it was angry.

"Are you sure someone went through your papers?" Peggy's tone was cajoling, as always, trying to keep everyone calm and at peace the way she always did. "You keep your office in such a mess, how can you tell if something is missing or has just been moved?"

I tried not to smile. Char's office was always a bit of a sore spot for Peggy. It was in one of the outbuildings, what had originally been built as a dower house for Arabella's mother. Char needed an office at Sea Oats, but thought having it in the main house wasn't a good idea—she liked separating home and work. Char wouldn't let anyone in the little house, not even to clean, and I knew what she was going to say before she said it.

"I know where everything is."

My heart was pounding so hard I could hear it in my ears. The sun went behind a cloud and I shivered—anticipation? Fear? Nerves? Some combination of all of them?

"I don't see how that's possible," Peggy insisted. "There's no way you could possibly. And why would someone be going through your office? What could they possibly want?"

"Information. You know someone is buying up our stock. And there are some other things going on that I'm concerned about. If you'd listen during board meetings, or read the minutes, you'd know these things." Char's voice was tense, tight.

If something was going on with the company—something major—then this was the worst possible time for me to be here.

I glanced around. There was nowhere to hide, and I didn't have enough time to run to the other side of the maze and get away.

No, I was a sitting duck out there in the open.

I couldn't decide whether I should stand and acknowledge I could hear them before they saw me, or to just sit there and wait for the doom coming.

They came around the side of the maze. Char's mouth was open. She was about to say something else when she saw me.

She scowled and walked hurriedly across the lawn toward me, the much shorter Peggy running to keep up.

I stayed seated and forced a smile on my face.

"What the hell are you doing here?" were the first words my wife spoke to me in almost two years.

Chapter Two

She hadn't changed much since I'd last seen her.

There might be just a few more strands of gray in the short auburn hair, cut in a thick bob framing the strong face. There might have been more lines around the always unreadable bluish-gray eyes, and maybe a couple of extra pounds on the imposing, athletic figure. But she looked good. She was tall, nearly five-ten, and was wearing a gray silk pantsuit over black sensible flats. She'd been a competitive rower in college, and making time for the gym was still clearly important to her. She wasn't pretty in a classic sense, but the strong chin and defiant cheekbones, combined with her unusual nose and wide mouth, were arresting, hard to look away from. She was a handsome woman who rarely bothered with makeup; she didn't need it. When she smiled, it was like someone turned on a spotlight behind her face. She glowed when she was happy, and that was when she was most attractive.

She wasn't smiling now. I wasn't sure if she'd already been scowling or if the scowl was for my benefit. In either case, she was *not* thrilled to see me.

I hadn't believed she'd spent the last two years pining for me, but her reaction was still kind of a letdown.

So many times I'd wondered what this moment would be like that now that it was here, happening, it seemed kind of anticlimactic. I don't know what I was expecting, but it wasn't this, whatever *this* was. My heart was racing, and I felt like an idiot.

I should have known. She'd made it clear she was finished with me the night I left. Wasn't that why I left, no matter how much I tried to convince myself I'd been wrong and should have stayed, should have fought for my marriage?

She hadn't filed for divorce because…well, I didn't know why, but it wasn't because she was hoping I'd come back.

That, at least, was clear.

I glanced over at Peggy, who was apparently not going to throw me a bone and confess to inviting me. She was doing some weird thing with her eyes, standing just behind Charlotte who couldn't see what she was doing, and I assumed she meant *Don't tell her I emailed you.*

Same old Peggy. Two years might have passed, but not a damned thing around here had changed.

I shrugged. "I came in with the tour, but got bored and wandered off. I mean, I've already heard everything the tour guide had to say about Sea Oats." I gestured limply around. "Nothing ever changes around here, does it?" I smiled at Peggy, who had the decency to blush.

"I told you," Charlotte said out of the side of her mouth to Peggy, "we'd regret letting those tours in the house."

That seemed to break whatever spell Peggy had been under. She laughed. "Don't be ridiculous, Char." Peggy held out her hands to me. "It's great to see you again, Ariel, and if you're with the tour, then we owe you some pastry and coffee, at the very least. It's included in the cost of the tour." She stepped toward me, and once Charlotte could no longer see her face she made an impossible to miss *follow my lead, please* look. She laughed again. "What a pleasant surprise, Ariel. I've missed you." She took my hands and helped me get to my feet, then whispered, "Play along," as she tucked my arm inside hers.

"I wouldn't want to impose." I glanced at Charlotte. Her face was, as always, unreadable, her arms crossed in front of her.

"No trouble at all!" Peggy said gaily, which was finally too much for Charlotte. She huffed angrily and spun on her heel, walking quickly away in the direction of the house. Once she was out of earshot, Peggy rolled her eyes. "Thanks for covering for me, Ariel."

"Well, I didn't think she'd approve of you getting in touch with me." I sighed. "Why did you email me, Peggy?"

"Why didn't you email me back? Or call? Let me know you were coming?"

I bit my lower lip. I didn't want to tell her that on one of those awful Saturday nights, after too much wine, I'd defiantly deleted the phone numbers for everyone at Sea Oats from my phone. And when I'd tried to call the main number for Sea Oats, I always hung up before anyone could answer.

"But I did email you," I replied as we started walking slowly. Peggy was a short woman, so I had to narrow my own steps to walk beside her. She was barely five feet tall, and although I knew her to be in her late forties, she looked much younger than her age. She was dressed casually, in a gray windbreaker thrown over her jeans and sweater. "I thought it was odd you never responded. I got concerned and decided to just come out here. You made it sound important. Was I wrong? Did I make a mistake in coming here?"

"No, I'm glad you're here." She smiled at me. "Charlotte won't admit it but I'm sure she's glad to see you, too."

"I wouldn't bet money on that," I replied, and we both laughed.

"There's a storm coming." She looked back over her

shoulder. The wind from the ocean was getting stronger. "You came in with the tour? Did you leave your car in the village?"

"No, I live in the city. I don't have a car. I took the train, and checked in to the inn," I replied. "You made it sound urgent. Was it not?"

It was the second time I'd asked, and the second time she didn't answer.

"How long can you stay?"

"I'm on vacation—I don't have to be back in the office until next week—"

"Oh, good, so you *can* stay awhile. I'll send someone to check you out and get your things." Peggy sounded absolutely thrilled, and she was smiling. "And when it's time to head home, Philip can drive you into the city, no need for you to take the train."

"I don't know if I'll stay that long," I said carefully. "Coming out here was more of an impulse than anything else."

"Oh, but you're here now, Ariel, and that's wonderful! Wonderful! More than I could have hoped for." She stopped and beamed at me, then gave me a big hug. She'd always given the best hugs. I closed my eyes. The smell of her perfume— Opium—brought back so many memories. "I'm so glad you're here, really, I am. You shouldn't have left, you know."

"I—"

"I'll let Karen know you're not going back with the tour and ask Maeve to bring up some pastries and coffee to the library, and let her know we'll have an extra at dinner and you'll be staying."

I hesitated. Charlotte hadn't exactly been encouraging. "Are you sure this is a good idea?" I couldn't trust Peggy Glaven completely. I'd made that mistake before. She was a lovely person, and I liked her a lot—but the family *always* came first with her.

And the family was Charlotte and her brother Sebastian.

"Charlotte—"

"Was caught off guard." She gave me yet another hug. "I know her, Ariel, and while she may not be willing to admit it just yet, she *was* glad to see you. Trust me."

Trust me.

What was I getting myself into?

If I was smart, I'd have gotten a cab and headed straight for the train station and never looked back.

"Give me a few minutes, and meet me in the library?" She started walking away, and then turned and looked back. "You do remember where the library is, don't you?" She winked before disappearing around the edge of the maze.

The wind was getting stronger, so I put my hood back up. I wasn't in a hurry to get back to the house—or to run into Charlotte again. I walked back to the fountain and sat down on the edge again with a sigh.

The storm was moving in quickly from out at sea, and the wind felt damp. It was going to pour, and just as I thought that I saw lightning flash in the distance.

I looked at my reflection in the water. Peggy didn't mention whether Bast was here or not.

Bast.

Bast was Sebastian, Charlotte's younger brother.

I'll cross that bridge when I get to it, I said to myself.

My mother always used to say "worrying was just borrowing trouble."

I shivered. But I had to face him, too.

And if my first encounter with Charlotte hadn't been encouraging, it hadn't exactly been *discouraging*, either. She hadn't ordered me off the property, and she'd seemed... preoccupied? What was it they'd been talking about? She'd been saying someone had searched her office, and someone was trying to take over Swann's? Like me, she could be single-minded about work. She'd been caught off guard, her mind was somewhere else, and she couldn't deal with me just then if something was going on with Swann's.

Yes, that *would* be her biggest concern. Swann's always came first with Charlotte. I hadn't liked taking a back seat to her company, especially after giving up my own career to come out to Sea Oats. I'd been stupid, yes, and not thinking clearly—running a worldwide company like Swann's wasn't easy, and I should have known it was going to take up a great deal of her time. And it wasn't fair for me to blame her for my decision to give up my career. She hadn't asked me to, had even, when I told her I was going to quit my job, asked me if I was sure I'd be happy not working. No, she'd been understanding—understood me even better than I understood myself.

There was probably some compromise that could have been made so I could have kept working. The thought had crossed my mind more than a few times over the last few years, if I was going to be honest with myself. Hollis had hated me resigning, and had been thrilled when I came back. So, no, she would have been willing to work something out with me.

God, what a fool I'd been.

I should have been more understanding.

The childish little voice in my head replied, *But she wasn't exactly very understanding of my needs, was she?*

I sighed and rolled my eyes. Maybe she hadn't been, but she had tried sometimes.

Which was more than I could say. I never tried. I was a willful, spoiled brat who wanted what I wanted and if Charlotte didn't give in I pouted and cried and acted like…like a child.

Not a wife.

How had she put up with me and my immaturities for so long?

It didn't take a psychologist to see that our marriage had been destined to fail from the beginning.

And if our marriage had worked out, I wouldn't have my current career. And I was pretty happy with where it was at right now. My future was promising. Soon to be a full partner, with all that entailed, with profit sharing and more of a support staff to handle the day-to-day, interns to train, new designers to mentor. And I had an eye for design, Hollis certainly thought so.

Yeah, terrific. My career couldn't hold me while I fell asleep at night, couldn't go with me to a movie, couldn't keep me company at dinner.

Hollis had been divorced three times. Her current husband was my age and she was putting him through medical school.

But if my personal life was a disaster, I was a success professionally, and well on my way to becoming one of the best interior designers in the country, if not the world, and that was something. I was the youngest interior designer to ever be featured in the *New York Times,* and that piece had brought in a lot of commissions for me and Hollis Allman Interior Designs.

And I had to face the truth about romance. My old ideas of what a relationship meant, what it was supposed to be, had been unrealistic and unworkable. I'd dreamed of a relationship like something out of the Disney cartoons my parents showed me when I was a kid. Charlotte was no Beast, I was no Belle, and Sea Oats wasn't an enchanted castle.

I was too young to give up on ever having a true partnership with another woman, but if it never happened for me—well, that was fine, too. I liked my apartment, I liked living alone, and I loved my job.

Anything else on top of that was just gravy.

But wanting some gravy wasn't asking too much, was it?

The way the sun was casting light underneath the dark clouds out at sea was gorgeous; the way it molded shadows from the bushes and even the fountain's waters triggered something in my creativity. I'd recently taken a commission to decorate an apartment on the Upper West Side, an enormous old place that the new owner wanted to completely modernize. The way the shadows, and the light, were combining to create patterns was something that just might work in the big living room with its big windowed river view, that would look gorgeous in the light from the setting sun.

I grabbed my phone out of my bag and unlocked it with the passcode quickly. I glanced over my apps—no text messages, forty-six new emails, but nothing on my social media. I took a moment to glance through the emails to make sure nothing pressing was there, and then switched over to my camera app.

I don't know what designers and artists used to do before the invention of the smartphone. I found myself taking pictures of furniture, color combinations, patterns and landscaping and crown moldings all the time. Whenever I was stuck on a project, I could scan through the thousands of images on my computer and find something that would trigger my creativity.

And the grounds at Sea Oats were spectacular—even that damned maze.

I stood up and started snapping pictures, turning a full 360 degrees in panorama mode, the screen on my phone whirring and clicking as picture after picture was taken. The clouds of the coming storm—there was a flash of lightning, forking down to the gray water—were also spectacular, and I kept turning, my finger snapping away. When I finished, I turned the phone back to sleep mode and dropped it back into my purse. I started walking back toward the house, wondering why precisely Peggy had wanted me to come.

Why now, after two years, had Peggy sent for me? What could possibly be going on around here that Peggy could have thought I could help the Swanns with?

Peggy was a cousin of sorts to Charlotte and her younger brother Bast. Her grandmother had been a Swann, which made them what? First cousins once removed? Second cousins? I've never figured out how to sort that sort of thing out, but that was how Peggy was related to them. She'd lived at Sea Oats for most of her life. Peggy was ten years older than Charlotte and had come to live with them when her own mother had died. In the nineteenth century, she would have been referred to as a poor relation. Charlotte and Bast were small children when Peggy arrived, and neither of them could remember a time when she hadn't been there. Peggy had devoted herself to both Charlotte and Bast from the moment she'd arrived. There was never any question about where her loyalties lay.

If she thought a reconciliation between Charlotte and me was the best thing for Charlotte, she would fight tooth and nail for us to make it work. If she thought Char was better off without me, she'd show me the door without a second thought, wipe off her hands and say good riddance, and I would cease to exist, as far as she was concerned.

Any expectations I might have about Peggy, and what she was up to, had to start with that unfortunate truth—I could only trust her to do what she thought was best for *them*. She'd never married, hadn't even gone to college. She'd stayed on at Sea Oats and helped raise them when their own mother had died only a few years after she arrived.

While I always saw her as more of a sister-like figure to Char and Bast, she kind of saw them as her own children—and

I wasn't completely convinced they didn't think of her as a mother.

With all that went along with that kind of feeling.

Charlotte had sometimes let it slip that she felt Peggy had spoiled Bast, made it possible for him to never grow up by making excuses for him—and excuses had always been necessary for Bast. I thought Charlotte had also probably spoiled Bast as much, if not more, than Peggy had. He was six years younger, so she'd always looked out for him and indulged him a little too much. There had been trouble with him in boarding school—I know he'd been kicked out of Phillips Exeter, and Charlotte always seemed to find an excuse for him. He'd flunked out of numerous colleges before finally giving up, and had never shown the least bit of interest in doing anything remotely resembling work for anyone, let alone Swann's. That had to disappoint Charlotte, who loved that department store chain like it was her own child. She couldn't understand why anyone else, especially a Swann, wouldn't feel the same way.

I'd wondered a few times—usually deep into a bottle of wine—whether things might have worked out differently if I'd asked her to give me a job at Swann's. I was an excellent designer, if still unproven at the time, and there had to be something I could have done with Swann's.

Even if I had just been designing the window displays, the work might have tied us closer together.

Instead of driving us further apart.

Yes, I'd been immature enough to be jealous of Swann's.

What a hopeless idiot I'd been.

I started walking back to the house. It would be strange staying at Sea Oats again, but I'd be lying if I said that I hadn't hoped Peggy would invite me to stay. That also meant Peggy knew Char wouldn't object too strenuously to my staying, which had to be a good sign, right?

Which also meant I had to admit I was still in love with her.

You're an idiot, I said to myself. The storm was getting closer. I could feel the rain in the air and smell it. I needed to get back to the house before it broke.

I'd used to love thunderstorms at Sea Oats, climbing to the top of the tower and sitting up there as rain raged and lightning flashed around me. It was probably not the smartest thing to do, but there were lightning rods on top of the house. One of our first arguments after I'd come here to live had been about watching a storm up there. Lightning made Charlotte uncomfortable—the theory was being struck by lightning was what caused the small plane her parents were on to crash—but I, of course, in my youth and insensitivity thought she was being overly cautious and ridiculous. Now I realize I should have humored her regardless of my own opinion—she was genuinely worried—but winning that small victory over her, asserting my independence, had seemed terribly important at the time. And she'd learned to live with my storm watching.

Or at least stopped bringing it up.

I had been insufferable. How had she put up with me?

"Miss Ariel! Miss Ariel!"

Startled, I jumped, my heart racing. Old Angus had emerged from the hedge maze without warning, and I'd been so lost in thought I didn't notice him until he spoke. "Angus! How are you?"

He looked…well, he didn't look good. He was old, maybe in his late sixties? He'd worked for the Swanns since he was a young man, just as his father had before him. The hedge maze was, of course, his pride and joy. I never let on to him how uncomfortable it made me, and he had taken a liking to me when I first came to Sea Oats, always bringing me fresh flowers he thought I'd like. But now he looked…well, not good. His eyes were bloodshot and bulging, and years of working in the sun and in the sea wind had worn deep creases in his darkened skin. He'd been balding when I'd lived here, and now his hair was all gone on the top, the pinkish skin burned by the sun and peeling. The hair on the sides of his head had gone completely white, and he was more bent over than he'd been before. His blue eyes looked wild, and he smelled slightly of stale tobacco and whiskey.

"Are you back for good, Miss Ariel?" He grabbed my arm with a dirty hand, the nails chewed down to the quick and lined with grime. His hand was strong, and I got a strong whiff of body odor.

"Just for a visit, Angus." I gently freed my arm from his grip. "Maybe a week or so. Are you all right?"

He grimaced at me. "You need to come back to stay, Miss Ariel. This is your home. This is where you belong." His eyes were darting back and forth nervously, like he was afraid we'd be overheard. "Although it's not as safe as it was."

"As safe?"

I stared at him. Angus had always liked a nip of whiskey now and then—no one minded, as long as his work didn't slip. He'd been around so long he was like a part of the family—no, that wasn't quite right. People always say that about servants, but people who work for you aren't like family. It was hard to imagine Sea Oats without Angus working on the grounds. He was a part of Sea Oats like Poseidon's Fountain, the swan pond, and the hedge maze. But clearly he was drinking more than he had, and maybe it was time for someone to have a word with him about it. Maybe I should ask Peggy. She ran

Sea Oats so Char and Bast didn't have to be bothered with any of those pesky housekeeping details.

"Are you all right, Angus? What do you mean by that? Maybe you should lie down for a bit."

He leaned in close to me and I tried not to wince at the smell. His face was covered in salt-and-pepper stubble, and if I didn't know him, I would have thought a bum had somehow gotten onto the property.

"Just remember, Miss Ariel, the center of the maze is where the truth lies."

"What?" Was he drunk? He was rank, but I couldn't smell any alcohol on him.

"Remember." He stepped back away from me and pointed a gnarled index finger at me. "Remember."

He walked away from me, and I was too confused to say or do anything other than watch him disappear around the corner of the maze. I started walking slowly back toward the house, thinking, *I need to talk to Peggy about Angus.* It was unfortunate, but he was not in his right mind. Maybe he was just drunk? No one would care, so long as Angus was capable of doing his job, and clearly, the grounds at Sea Oats had never looked better.

I took out my phone again and started taking more pictures. No weeds to be seen anywhere, the grass a full lush green, the flowers budding in their meticulous beds. I went in the back door to the house and up the back staircase just off the kitchen. I could smell coffee and fresh pastries, heard the murmur of voices talking behind the closed door. I caught some French—so the tour group was now in the kitchen.

The back stairs were narrow and I hadn't switched on the lights, so it was dark in there as well. The stairs were originally only for the use of the servants and had never been modernized;

the family and guests used the main staircase in the front of the house, and as such the back stairs weren't exactly the safest, easiest staircase to go up or down. The master bedroom suite I'd shared with Char when I lived here was much closer to these stairs, so I'd become well acquainted with them, going up and down them several times a day. The concept of having servants was alien to me. I was not to the manor born, and it took me a while to get used to having people pick up after me and cook and clean for me.

I'd be lying, though, if I said I didn't miss that after I moved back to the city. There were so many times, as I washed dishes and vacuumed my little apartment, that I wished I had Maeve to do it for me! I worked long hours at my job, often grabbing takeout on my way home from the office, so exhausted both mentally and physically that I left everything for the weekend, switching on the television, binge-watching something on Netflix or Hulu to distract my mind from being so tired. And then, of course, that meant I spent the weekend getting caught up on things and before I knew it, Monday had rolled around again and it was time to get back to work.

I'd lost myself in my work, given myself to it completely, so I wouldn't think about Char, wonder what she was doing, why she hadn't come after me, why I was so lonely without her, why I had so stupidly ruined things, why I had just run away rather than fighting for our marriage.

And I was good at my job, very good at my job. The irony, of course, is that was how we'd met: Char had hired the firm I worked for to redecorate the offices at Swann corporate headquarters. It was my first big job. I was just out of the New York School of Interior Design. I'd managed to land an internship with Hollis Allman, one of the top designers in the city, and she'd liked my work enough to offer me a job when I graduated. It was a great opportunity, and I worked very hard for Hollis, who was not an easy boss. She didn't put up with incompetence—hell, she didn't put up with much of anything other than thorough professionalism. She'd given me the Swann job, and I was pretty determined to do a great job.

After that initial meeting, my contact with Charlotte was minimal. I primarily worked with her personal assistant, Carole Berry. Carole was a ruthlessly efficient woman in her fifties whose bluntness—to the point of rudeness—I gradually began to appreciate. There was nothing passive-aggressive about Carole Berry; she knew what her boss wanted and she refused to waste time not coming to the point. I soon learned to be direct with her, and to push back, earning her respect. I usually only saw Charlotte in passing—when she vacated her office so I could take some measurements, walking briskly through the office with files in hand, her glasses perched on top of her head. In those first few weeks, I found myself trying to arrange my time at Swann's to when I could be reasonably sure she would be there. I was feeling a strong pull toward her. I'd never been drawn to older women before—the occasional mild crush on one of my professors in college was about it, and those had always passed relatively quickly—and I couldn't help but notice there were no personal pictures in her office, nothing to make it more homey and less businesslike, no pictures of a husband or children or family.

I don't remember how long it took me to start Googling Charlotte, trying to get an idea—any idea—of a personal life. I found out a lot about her family, the history of Swann's, the big house out on Long Island, but very little about her. She'd never married, never been linked in gossip columns to anyone. That didn't mean she was a lesbian, of course—it could just mean she was very private.

But I found myself fantasizing about her, daydreaming what it would be like to be with her, to see those grayish-blue eyes sparkle with delight when seeing me, walking through Central Park holding hands together, candlelit dinners and concerts and plays, cuddling in the backseat of a cab, wondering what it would feel like to be held in her strong arms, to be kissed by those full lips, how her mouth would feel on my body.

I tried to hide it, of course—it was the epitome of unprofessional. Hollis had a zero-tolerance policy for fraternizing with clients. And I figured so long as I never acted on my attraction, on my fantasies for her, everything would be fine. I mean, I was barely out of the closet. My first experience had been in college, when I was still dating men halfheartedly, allowing people to set me up with brothers and friends and roommates of friends and friends of cousins.

Once I was finished with school, I was finished with men, too. But I hadn't had much luck since going to work for Hollis—I wouldn't just have sex with someone for the sake of having sex, and none of the women I met, the women I dated—it just wasn't there for me. I wasn't sure if Charlotte was a lesbian, but I was attracted to her, fantasized about her when I daydreamed, but knew when the job was done I'd probably never see her again.

Charlotte waited until the job was finished before asking me out.

Three months later we were married.

Marry in haste, repent at leisure.

I walked down the hallway to the library. The library at Sea Oats had always been my favorite room in the house. It was two enormous rooms, one on top of the other, with a metal spiral staircase leading from the second floor library to the third. As I approached, the door opened and Maeve came out, shutting the door behind her.

I'd always liked Maeve. She was Angus's cousin, I

think—their family had been in service at Sea Oats going back decades. She was younger than Angus, and she smiled warmly at me, bowing her head slightly. "Nice to see you, Miss Ariel."

I'd never gotten used to be calling *Miss*, but all the servants insisted and I'd long ago given up trying to get them to stop. "Maeve! You're looking well."

"I sent Joseph into town to collect your things and settle up your bill, Miss. Miss Peggy is waiting for you in the library. Had I known you were coming, I would have made some blueberry muffins." She smiled. "But I'll make some for your breakfast."

"You're too good to me, Maeve." She was an incredible cook. I'd gained ten pounds living at Sea Oats—ten pounds that had been very hard to find the time to take off once I'd moved back to the city.

I'd be more careful this time.

I watched her walk down the hallway to the back stairs before I opened the library door and went inside to meet my fate.

CHAPTER THREE

The library was always my favorite room in the house.

Samuel Swann had built Sea Oats to please his young second wife, Arabella Sturdevant. Arabella, the last of a long line of Sturdevants going back to the original Dutch settlers of New Amsterdam, not only liked fine art but was also an avid reader and loved books. She'd also donated a lot of money to the New York Public Library and had provided the money for the creation and building of the Penobscot Library. Arabella's passion for books, for literacy, was something she had passed along to her descendants. Every Swann's department store had a book section, and ten percent of the book sales were earmarked for local library donations.

Like Arabella, I loved books and I loved reading. My earliest memories were of reading books, and the first time I saw the library at Sea Oats it was like one of my fondest dreams had come true. My little apartment in the city was, even now, crammed full of books, and I tried to spend at least an hour a day before bed reading.

The library at Sea Oats was enormous. It ran around the front corner of the house, encompassing the round tower with the witch's hat atop, and the spiral staircase running up to the higher level was in a corner of the tower. There wasn't a ceiling dividing the room into separate floors, but up on the third floor a wide gallery ran around the room. The tower had enormous windows, and there was also a skylight above, so there was plenty of natural sunlight in the room. Every inch of the walls where there was no window was covered with floor to ceiling bookshelves—and since the ceilings were sixteen feet high, there was a lot of room for a lot of books. On the second floor, there was plush, thick green carpeting and enormous wooden reading tables, as well as comfortable armchairs to sit in.

Above the fireplace on the second floor was an enormous John Singer Sargent painting of Arabella.

I'd always thought the painting belonged in a museum. It was worth a fortune, but the room would almost seem empty without it. There were other paintings of Arabella in the house, of course, but this was the only one that made her seem like an actual person who'd lived and breathed in the house.

I'd always felt a strange kinship with Arabella. We were nothing alike—she was a society heiress from New York City, had been given a remarkable education by her parents, and, of course, had married a man and been a wife and mother as well as a philanthropist.

I was born in the Midwest to middle-class parents and grew up in nondescript suburbs and went to public schools— managing to escape for college to New York.

I was also a lesbian.

But we'd both been Swann wives, and there was something about her kind face—a kindness present in all the paintings of her—that made me think we might have been friends had we known each other. She looked like the kind of woman who inspired confidences, was loyal and a good friend. Loving to read as I did, I spent a lot of time in Arabella's library. None of Arabella's books, of course, were still on the shelves—they were now valuable and the collection had been donated years ago to the New York Public Library, where her voluminous correspondence and diaries were also stored. Charlotte and Sebastian's mother had also been a devotee of reading, and she was the one who'd cataloged and donated Arabella's collections, as well as updated the Sea Oats library. The library was badly in need of another update—Charlotte didn't have a lot of time to read anything besides sales reports and analyses, Bast didn't read at all, and I don't remember ever seeing Peggy with a book—and so there wasn't anything on the shelves more recent than the early 1990s. Some of the older books were probably collector's items, and many of them were signed first editions.

I'd considered taking on cataloging and updating the library when I'd lived here, but it was such an enormous project I'd been a little daunted. I'd mentioned it to Charlotte, who suggested hiring someone to do it, like a professional librarian or cataloger. She was probably right, but it still stung a little. I was insulted she didn't think I was competent to do it myself, which in retrospect wasn't what she'd been saying at all. But as a result I'd lost interest in the project—either doing it myself or hiring someone to do it—and in my absence it was safe to assume no one else had done it, either.

There was a fire going in the fireplace when I opened the door and walked in. Sea Oats was, like many old houses, drafty and hard to keep warm, so the fire was welcome as the temperature was dropping because of the incoming storm.

The enormous heavy green velvet draperies were pulled back from the windows in the tower, held in place with gold braid ending in enormous tassels. The sky was darkening and filling with dark clouds—the storm would break over the house soon. I involuntarily shivered. Two matching wingback beige chairs had been arranged in front of the fireplace, and the silver coffee service was set up on one of the antique side tables placed between the two chairs. There was a plate piled high with pastries, a butter dish, and a small china bowl of raspberry jam. My stomach growled. I hadn't eaten anything other than a couple of glazed doughnuts I'd grabbed to have with my coffee that morning at a Dunkin' Donuts in Penn Station, and had skipped lunch.

Peggy was already sipping coffee from a delicate china cup. I plopped down in the other wingback chair and reached for a croissant, liberally smeared it with both butter and jam. I poured myself a cup of coffee and wolfed down the croissant. The pastry was still warm.

No one made croissants better than Maeve's.

"It must feel strange to be back here," Peggy observed as I started working on a second croissant. "I sent Joseph in to settle your bill and collect your things. I'm going to put you in the green room, if that's all right with you?"

The green room was on the third floor, just down the hall from the tower. The family bedrooms were all on the second floor, and while I certainly hadn't expected to be put back in the suite I'd shared with Charlotte, being put up on the guest floor made my status at Sea Oats clear.

I was a guest, no longer family.

"That's fine," I replied, hoping my hurt feelings didn't show, while chiding myself inwardly for being hurt. *You aren't a part of the family anymore, get over it. You walked out two years ago, what do you expect? Only a legal technicality keeps you tethered to the Swanns.* "Why did you send for me? Why am I here, Peggy?"

"Don't you think it's time you dealt with things?" Peggy didn't look at me, kept her eyes focused on the flames. "Both you and Charlotte have been avoiding dealing with your situation for far too long. You both need to decide what you're going to do." She waved a hand. "This stasis you're both in— it's not productive for either of you."

"But why now?" I was curious. Peggy's loyalties were always going to lie with Charlotte and Sebastian. "I left two years ago, and not a word from you, from anyone. So what's so special about now?"

This time Peggy looked me in the eyes. "Charlotte has been seeing Lindsay Moore again."

I inhaled sharply.

Lindsay Moore.

I might have known.

Lindsay Moore was an ex of Charlotte's—*the* ex, really. Lindsay and Charlotte had grown up together, had known each other all their lives. Lindsay's family wasn't quite as moneyed as the Swanns—not many are—but it was old money, just the same. It was Lindsay's ancestor who'd suggested to Samuel that he build his new wife a house outside of Penobscot. The Moores and the Swanns went hand in hand, had even intermarried a few times, but never in the direct line, so Lindsay and Charlotte weren't related. I think the Moores made their money in textiles, but the businesses were long gone. Lindsay was the last of her family, and she was a lady who lunched rather than worked. I think she might have tried being a real estate agent, maybe even still was. I'd never gotten to know her well.

She'd hated me on sight, of course.

Charlotte and Lindsay had been romantically involved when they were teenagers at the same boarding school, and had even gone to Vassar together. I never really knew the whole story—Charlotte wouldn't talk about her, which I always took as a bad sign—so most of what I knew about Lindsay came from Bast and Peggy. Peggy wasn't a fan, since she'd hurt Charlotte, and I could never be certain that Bast was telling me the truth about anything; he lied as easily as he breathed.

Whatever the truth was, something happened the summer

after they graduated from college, and Lindsay had married a man, a soap actor. That marriage had been an utter disaster, and only lasted a few years. Once she was safely divorced and back living in her house on the other side of Penobscot, Lindsay and Charlotte had gotten back together again. But she had also married twice more—both times to men—and the volatility of the Lindsay-Charlotte dynamic was one of those love/hate on-again/off-again things movies and television shows make look like the real thing, *true love*.

Because of course everyone falls in love with someone they can't stand.

Then again, the divorce rate is over fifty percent.

Lindsay had divorced her most recent husband, according to Bast, about six or seven months before Charlotte met me, and had been desperately trying to get things patched up with her again—sending her flowers, little gifts, dropping in at Sea Oats on the weekends unannounced and uninvited. Nothing seemed to work this time, though—Charlotte was wise to all the little tricks Lindsay had always used to get her back, and she wasn't falling for them again.

And then she married me.

I couldn't blame Lindsay for hating me. I knew if I were in her place, it would be hard for me to be pleasant to the person who'd married the person I considered my true love.

I guess I shouldn't have been surprised to hear that they were back together again. The real surprise was that it took this long to happen, and I said as much.

I said it lightly, like I didn't care, but my heart sank down into my shoes and it took all my self-control not to head back into the city.

What had I been thinking, coming out here?

I had expected to come to Sea Oats, see Charlotte, and fall back into her loving arms again. That was the blunt, hard truth.

I felt like an idiot for even daring to hope.

"Lindsay is all wrong for Char," Peggy replied. "She always has been. She'll just hurt her again."

Lindsay had been the master of the passive-aggressive insult. She might not be Swann-rich anymore, but she had that snobby boarding-school bitch thing going for her. She knew exactly how to make me feel like an idiot from the Midwest, who didn't know good wine from bad, which fork was for what, what soup went with what meat course, and the proper dessert, and all those little things rich girls are taught from childhood so it becomes second nature for them. She always made me feel like I didn't know how to dress, like I was some big clumsy oaf, a bull in a china shop, saying something cutting and rude to me that sounded perfectly innocuous to someone else.

And every time I saw her, I couldn't help but wonder what Charlotte saw in *me*.

Then again, Charlotte *had* loved me enough to marry me at one time. That had to be galling for Lindsay—and it must have been even harder for her to be polite to me.

"Is that why you invited me out here," I asked slowly, "to come between them? That's kind of melodramatic, isn't it? It's like something out of *The Young and the Restless*."

Peggy threw back her head and laughed. Wiping at her eyes, she said, "Oh, Ariel, I've missed you so much." She got a hold of herself again and leaned over, lowering her voice. "I won't say that I'm thrilled Char is seeing her again. But I'm most definitely not trying to interfere in her love life. I would never do that."

"Good," I replied. "Because I wouldn't do that, Peggy. Not for you, not for anyone."

"Not even for yourself, Ariel?"

"Not even for me," I replied after a moment. It wasn't the

first time it occurred to me that I had been, in fact, the other woman; Lindsay had certainly pointed it out to me enough times for me to get her point. When no one else was around to hear her, of course. That wasn't how Lindsay operated. She was like one of the mean girls in high school, sniping from the sidelines rather than being direct. I've always preferred being direct to subterfuge, even when subterfuge was the smarter course to take. Complaining about Lindsay to Charlotte didn't do me any good, which of course, didn't help my feelings of insecurity.

Charlotte saying *I married you, didn't I?* was not the help she thought it was.

"Then why did you come?" Peggy asked. "After all this time?"

"Because you emailed me and asked me to come." I struggled to get my phone out of my pocket so I could read her the email out loud. When I finished, I added, "After reading that, how could I not come?"

"I was a bit melodramatic, wasn't I?" She placed her coffee cup back down in the saucer. "I didn't mean to worry you, but things here are different now than when you lived here."

I remembered Charlotte's words about her office being searched. "What is going on, Peggy? You can tell me."

"Well, for one thing." She held up her hand. The ring on her finger caught the light and flashed multicolored fire.

"Is that...an engagement ring?"

She nodded, smiling.

"But who?" I goggled at her. As far as I knew, Peggy had never been involved with anyone. I couldn't have been the only person who assumed she'd never marry.

"Roger asked me, and I said yes."

"Roger *Stanhope*?" I hoped my voice didn't sound as shocked as I felt.

I knew Roger, of course. He was a very successful investment banker, and an old family friend. When the Swanns had taken the company public years ago, he had handled the entire thing for them, making a small fortune for himself in the process. I'd always liked Roger—he was very kind to me, always willing to talk, and he had a smaller house on the outskirts of Penobscot, usually coming out for the weekends. He was an attractive older man, played regular tennis to keep fit. He'd been married once before, but his wife had been killed in a car accident and he'd never remarried.

"Congratulations," I finally managed to say. I'd never imagined Roger and Peggy as a couple, and even now, I couldn't see it. She was so devoted to Char and Bast, and the house!

She put her hand down again. "We've gotten close over the last year, and when he asked me, how could I say no?" She gestured around the room. "I'll miss living here, of course, but..." She hesitated. "It's past time for me to go. I should have moved out of here years ago. It's Char's and Bast's house, after all." She shook her head. "But Roger is ready to retire, and we're going to be doing a lot of traveling."

And then it hit me—why she'd wanted me to come. *She* was going to be leaving, and she wanted to make sure both Charlotte and Bast were settled before she went.

"You know all I want is for Charlotte to be happy." She looked back at the fire. "I don't believe Lindsay will make her happy. You made her happy, Ariel. I've never seen Charlotte as happy as when you were living here. And she's not been happy since you left."

That admission was an enormous betrayal for her. I shook

my head. "I appreciate that, Peggy. But that's over now. I've accepted it, and I'm sure Charlotte has, too."

"But you're here, you came! So you still care, don't you? Don't you want to make this all work out? I know you still love her, Ariel—it's all over your face."

"I—I don't know how I feel." I wasn't lying to her. I had pushed it all so far down inside for so long…and seeing her again brought up a lot of feelings I thought, or rather convinced myself, I'd been certain were gone. My hand shook as I poured myself some more coffee. It was perfect, strong and hot the way Maeve always made it. I'd missed that.

I'd missed so much more.

But I wasn't going to get my hopes up.

What we had was over.

"You know Lindsay's wrong for her," Peggy went on.

"And what about Bast?" I heard myself saying. It was the elephant in the room and it needed addressing. "Is he here?"

Peggy didn't miss a beat. "He's coming in from the city this evening," she replied. "His fiancée is staying here already. She's right down the hall from you, in the red room."

Sebastian.

I couldn't very well face the past without facing Sebastian. He was why I'd run away in the first place.

Sebastian, or Bast as we called him, was Charlotte's younger brother. He was her opposite in every way. From earliest childhood Charlotte was interested in Swann's, wanted to go to work there, and studied hard so she could learn how to run the company one day. Bast, on the other hand…he was such the wastrel playboy trust-fund brat, he was almost a stereotype. Charlotte and Peggy finally gave up on him getting a college education when he was twenty and decided the best way for him to make a living was as a celebrity of sorts, which apparently meant getting his picture in the tabloids and making scenes at parties and then getting paid to show up for parties and being asked to model here and there and some other things I never quite understood. I'd known who Bast Swann was long before I met his sister—he was kind of like a male Paris Hilton, always in the tabloids, always doing something crazy. He was nothing like Charlotte. They had an odd relationship for siblings—Char was deeply protective of him, but at the same time the way he lived his life sometimes pushed her to the limits.

As a Swann, he had some voting percentage of the company and he wasn't above using that as leverage to get access to the money in the family trust, which Char was the trustee of. Char had explained it all to me once, how it all worked, but it confused me then and I'm still not entirely sure I grasp it. Everything was wrapped up in separate trusts—Sea Oats, for example, had its own separate trust—and the family money was in another, and there was another for the charity work, another for the company. I wasn't sure how many there were, if I was going to be honest. Managing my own money was enough of a challenge for me to deal with, and the complicated trusts Charlotte's grandfather had set up to protect everything were too much for me to wrap my mind around.

Besides, I didn't need to know all the details.

Char was chair of the trusts; even though she was young when their parents died, their parents were quite aware that Char was the responsible one and the best person for the job. They were managed for her before she turned twenty-five and took over control, not only of the trusts, but of Swann's. Bast had never married, and his love life was tabloid fodder—he had a penchant for misbehaving in public, and for young starlets. Bast loved his sister, but there was also an element of competitiveness there with him as well. It couldn't have been easy growing up with such a driven and intelligent older sister and to always be compared negatively to her. People expected Bast to be a wastrel, and he lived up to those expectations for him. I kind of felt sorry for him.

At first.

Bast was kind to me when I first came to Sea Oats, which I greatly appreciated. He was always willing to give me a sympathetic ear whenever Lindsay had said something that upset me, when Charlotte couldn't be bothered with what she called the junior high school theatrics of it all. Bast kept me company when I was lonely with Char in the city, taking it upon himself to teach me the family history and show me around Penobscot.

It never occurred to me that Bast's kindness was just a façade, a game he was playing to earn my trust. He didn't see me as a friend, or as family. Bast saw me as another pawn in the game he'd been playing with his sister since they were children. So, *of course* every time Char and I had an argument or a disagreement or I had another fit of jealousy about Lindsay, Bast was there with a shoulder for me to cry on, to comfort me and tell me I wasn't wrong to dislike Lindsay or feel unappreciated and ignored by Charlotte.

It never occurred to me once, in my unbelievable stupidity and naïveté, to question why Bast was being so kind to me, why Bast was always there for me, why he made such an effort to fill in for Charlotte in keeping me company while she was in the city at work. It never crossed my mind that he saw my boredom as another way to twist the knife in Charlotte, to punish her for whatever he wanted to get even with her for at the time. I didn't know that he was saying things to her about me, making her suspicious of my feelings for him—which were never more than friendship, ever—making her question whether I might not...

That I might not leave her for a man someday.

Yes, Bast knew Charlotte's weaknesses, knew that the one thing she'd never been able to get past with Lindsay was that Lindsay had left her and married a man—three times.

And the fear I would do the same thing was always in the back of her mind.

Bast played us both like fiddles, and made fools out of both of us.

So, of course, the night Charlotte and I had yet another blowout about Lindsay, of course the person I ran crying to was Bast. I've wondered sometimes, in the two years since, if Lindsay hadn't deliberately provoked me into that quarrel, if she and Bast hadn't been working together to get rid of me.

When you're alone in your apartment with nothing more than a bottle of wine and regrets, it's easy to see conspiracies where they don't exist.

And yet…everything had played out perfectly for the two of them if that had in fact been their endgame.

"I really don't have time for this," Charlotte said to me at the height of my anger, tears running down my face, waving her hand wearily, dismissing me like my feelings were childish and meant nothing to her and she was tired of having to deal with my silliness. "We can talk about this more, if you like, but only when you've calmed down and stopped acting like a child."

Had Charlotte been trying to push every insecurity button I had about our marriage, she couldn't have been more successful.

Somehow, I managed to get myself under control and, dramatically wiping the tears from my eyes, said, "I'm so sorry to have bothered you. But don't worry. It won't happen again." I turned and left our shared bedroom, slamming the door so hard the paintings on the hallway walls shook.

I stood there, my hand on the doorknob, close to

hyperventilating, wounded to the core and trying so hard not to start crying again.

She doesn't love me, she'd rather be with Lindsay, we both made a huge mistake, she wouldn't care if I left.

I don't really remember walking down the hallway. My memory is kind of vague. I know I was stumbling, almost fell once or twice, had my hand out against the wall to steady myself as I staggered down the second-floor hallway. I do remember that Bast's door was open, and he was standing in the doorway, a sympathetic look on his face. "Are you all right?" he asked in a very quiet voice. "I can't believe how cruel Charlotte was being to you."

It didn't occur to me until much later—too late—that the only way he could have heard us was to stand outside our bedroom door. Sea Oats was built solid, and his room was too far away for him to even have been aware that we were arguing, let alone what either of us had said.

"Am I crazy?" I asked, my voice shaky, the tears starting to form in my eyes again. "Why can't she understand how hard it is on me for her to be friends with Lindsay? Why can't she just understand and stop acting like I'm some stupid little girl?"

"There, there." Bast pulled me to him, and put his arms around me, kissing the top of my head while I gave in to the sobs, my entire body shaking with them as he stroked my back, murmuring soothing sounds to calm me down.

And it was like every frustration, every problem, every little thing that had bothered me since I moved to Sea Oats came bubbling up to the surface, and I couldn't stop sobbing. I couldn't stop thinking, wondering, wishing it was Charlotte who was comforting me, putting her arms around me, understanding and caring.

Why wasn't it Charlotte?

And after what seemed like hours, I was cried out. I was spent, so tired, emotionally and physically exhausted, still angry but the flames had died down considerably. I started to pull away from him, saying, "Oh, thank you, Bast—"

And he pulled me back into him and kissed me.

On the lips.

I was stunned, startled, didn't know what to do. I remember thinking, *What the hell?* and freezing. I didn't kiss him back, of course, but I didn't know what to do at first.

It had been a long time since I'd had to push a man off me.

Then the anger began to bubble up. I was bringing my hands up to violently push him away from me when Charlotte—surely regretting her angry words and how we'd left things, had come after me, perhaps to apologize, to make things right with me—had cleared her throat.

I spun around and saw her, her eyes narrow, her face white with fury, her lips compressed into a thin line. "Well," she said coldly, "isn't this a pretty picture?" She turned and walked back down the hallway toward our bedroom.

And Bast started laughing.

I spun around, and directed my humiliation and my anger at him. "You," was all I could get out as I slapped him across the face as hard as I could, the sound of the slap hanging in the air, the look of amusement on his face transitioning quickly to shock and then naked hatred, and in that moment I realized Bast had never been my friend, never, and he hated me and wanted me gone, had set me up with his kindness, played me for an utter fool.

If I'd had a gun in my hand, I would have gladly shot him dead right then and there.

Instead, I turned and ran after Char, calling her name, but she refused to answer me, speak to me. After I shut our bedroom door behind me, sobbing, trying to get the words out, trying to make her understand it wasn't what it looked like, she ignored me, wouldn't let me put my arms around her, wouldn't let me even touch her. The way she flinched away from me in revulsion was something I'd never forgotten, would probably never forget.

And when she finally did speak, her voice was cold. "You need to leave," she said. "Pack your things and go. Stay in a hotel, get an apartment, I don't care where you go. You just can't be here anymore. We're finished."

And she walked out of the room, slamming the door behind her with a finality.

I cried for about another minute or two, and then got angry.

She thought I would do that? With her *brother*?

What kind of person did she think I was?

So I packed and made a reservation at a hotel for a week. Joseph drove me into the city, and my mind was made up. I was never going back to Sea Oats unless she begged me to come back to her.

I was going to make it on my own. I would use the credit cards—she owed me that much at least—until I had a job and a place to live.

But deep down, I always believed she would come for me. Joseph knew what hotel I'd gone to, which was one of the reasons I had him take me. But by the third day, it became obvious to me she wasn't going to come, that she believed I was the kind of woman who not only would cheat on her, but would do it with her brother.

It was a slap in the face.

That's when I got good and angry.

I called Hollis and got my job back, spent the rest of the week finding an apartment I could afford on my salary, and once I got my first paycheck, I cut up every one of the credit cards Charlotte had given me and mailed the pieces back to her at Sea Oats. I cleared out the contacts in my cell phone and started my life over.

But a small part of me always kept hoping she'd come for me, despite everything.

Which was why I refused any dates, refused coworkers' offers to set me up with friends. I worked and I went home, watched movies and read books, went to museums and theater events. I didn't mind it, really, being alone.

"I wasn't aware Bast was engaged," I replied. "I'm very happy for him. It's way past time for him to settle down, isn't it?"

"Well." Peggy made a face. No one could be ever be good enough for Bast, as far as Peggy was concerned. She'd spoiled and indulged him when he was a little boy, and sometimes it seemed like she still thought of him as a little boy she needed to spoil and indulge. "She's a model."

She said it in the same tone she would have said, *She has the plague.*

"I haven't seen him linked to anyone lately."

"He says they've been keeping a low profile because it's the real thing." Peggy stood up. "Her name is Kayla. She seems harmless, I suppose, if you like the type. If you want to relax, you can go on up to your room—I need to go check on dinner. Joseph will bring your things up when he gets back from the inn. Dinner will be around seven. That should give you enough time to get settled in."

"Thanks." I got up and kissed her cheek. "But is everything all right, Peggy? I couldn't help overhearing you and Charlotte talking…"

"Oh, that." She waved her hand. "Yes, this may not be the best time for you to be here. Charlotte is—"

Whatever she was going to say next was cut off by the library doors bursting open and Maeve, her face pale and trying to catch her breath, standing there. "Pardon me, Miss Peggy, but it's Angus."

"What about him?" I asked, standing up.

"I'm afraid..." Her lips were quivering. "Oh, miss, I'm afraid he's dead."

CHAPTER FOUR

B ut I just saw him," was all I could say, stupidly, like my
seeing him out on the grounds somehow negated what
Maeve was telling us.

Maeve's eyes were red, and her hands were shaking. *Of
course, she's related to Angus*, I thought, as Peggy took control
in her usual, ruthlessly efficient way.

"Maeve, have a seat," she said, taking her by the arm and
leading her over to one of the chairs we'd just vacated. "Are
you okay?" Her voice was kind.

Maeve nodded, but didn't say anything for a moment,
wiping at her eyes with the back of her hands. She took a deep
breath and visibly got a hold of herself. "I've already called
for an ambulance and for the police, Miss Peggy. They're on
their way."

"The police?" Peggy shot a glance at me.

Maeve nodded. "Someone—he—oh, Miss Peggy!" She
burst into tears, covering her face with her hands. Peggy
rubbed her arm gently, murmuring something comforting in a
calm, quiet voice I couldn't hear.

I walked over to the windows in the tower section of
the library. The windows faced the driveway, and I could see
the tour van, still parked out there but out of the way. I could
hear sirens in the distance. As Maeve continued to sob, she

tried speaking at the same time. The gist of it was one of the groundkeepers had gone out to turn off Poseidon's Fountain and drain it a little before the storm hit—standard procedure, I remembered, whenever there was a storm, to keep the fountain from overflowing—and he came across Angus's body.

He'd been hit over the head with something—there was a massive wound on the back of his head and blood everywhere.

The body was near the entrance to the maze, right around where I'd seen him.

The center of the maze is where the truth lies. Remember, Miss Ariel, remember.

I shivered as I watched the flashing lights of the ambulance draw closer and finally pull up in front of the house. A couple of EMTs got out quickly and went up the front steps, and a few moments later a police car pulled up behind the ambulance.

"They're here, Peggy," I called, walking back over to where they were both sitting. Maeve got to her feet, using her apron to wipe her face dry. "I'll go down," she said. "I can't trust Allie to deal with them."

"One of the maids," Peggy said, seeing the puzzled look on my face. "I'd better go down and see what they need from me." She shook her head. "You may as well go wait in your room—I would imagine they're going to want to talk to you."

"Me?"

"You may have been the last person to see him alive, Ariel," she said as she closed the library door behind her.

I sank back down into the chair I'd been sitting in earlier. I poured myself another cup of coffee. There were a few pastries left, but my appetite was long gone. I felt a little like I'd been punched in the stomach. It didn't seem real.

I walked out into the hallway and climbed the stairs up to the third floor. The green room was near the library, but instead I walked down toward the french doors leading to a small balcony that faced the sea, where the hallway turned to the left at a ninety-degree angle. I opened the doors and walked out onto the balcony. The wind was cold and even damper than when I came in, and the sky was covered in dark clouds. The omnipresent hedge maze stretched out green and malevolent, and I could see the fountain was still on—the groundskeeper had understandably forgotten to turn it off. As I watched, the EMTs were led along the pathway to where Angus's body lay, facedown in the grass. I felt the coffee burning like acid in my stomach and I went back inside, leaning against the wall while I took deep breaths, trying to get myself back under control again.

Angus had always been kind to me when I lived here, I thought as I walked down the corridor to my room. He always brought me flowers from the gardens for my room, answered whatever questions I might have about the grounds, no matter how stupid, and no matter what he was doing. He'd made me feel welcomed, even more so than Maeve and the other staff. He didn't even seem to mind my aversion to the maze after that horrible time I got lost in there, even though it was his own personal obsession. "I don't know what we're going to do about the maze once Angus retires," Charlotte had told me once. "It's not like hedge maze experts are a dime a dozen in the United States. We might even have to finally dig it up if we can't find someone to maintain it properly."

Which was fine with me—but I'd never say that out loud.

I went to my room and checked my email until there was a light knock on the door. I looked up to see a very young-looking police officer standing there, his face red. "Miss Montgomery?" he asked, not quite able to look me in the eyes. "I'm Officer Abbott, and I—"

"You need to ask me some questions?" I asked, getting up from the bed.

"If you don't mind?" He blushed even deeper.

He was tall, well over six feet tall, and reedy, with long gangly arms and legs and narrow shoulders. His blondish hair was cut close to the scalp. His face was all angles and planes: sharp cheekbones, hollowed-in cheeks, thin lips, and a chin so pointed it could cut paper. There were some sandy chest hairs escaping from the top of his blue uniform shirt, where the top button wasn't fastened. His pants were too big for him, the black belt cinched tightly.

"I don't mind." He asked me for my full name and address and phone number, which I provided, and then asked why I was there. "I'm married to Charlotte Swann," I replied.

I hadn't thought it was possible for him to turn redder, but I'd been wrong. He scribbled down everything I said, not looking at me. "I understand you saw Angus McPherson before his untimely death?"

"I did, yes." I recounted to him everything I could remember about seeing Angus, and his cryptic words to me.

"So Ms. Glaven and Ms. Swann had already left before you saw Mr. McPherson?"

"Yes."

"The center of the maze is where the truth lies."

"Yes, that's what he said to me."

"And you don't know what he meant by that?"

"I thought—to be honest, I thought he'd been drinking." I held up my hands. "I know he used to drink sometimes while he was working. But that could have changed. I've not lived here for two years."

"Ms. Glaven had mentioned that. You just turned up today?"

"I didn't kill Angus," I replied, evenly. "And yes, I just turned up today."

He flipped his notebook closed. "Thank you, Ms. Montgomery. Someone else from the department may want to talk to you—I'm not in charge of the investigation—so we're going to have to ask you to not leave, at least for a few days."

"So it's murder, then?"

He nodded. "Someone bashed him in the head with a shovel, it looks like. We won't know for sure until the coroner checks him out, but it seems pretty obvious."

"I can't promise how long I can stay. I live and work in the city—"

"Just check in with us if you decide to head back into the city." He smiled at me, the red finally seeming to fade from his face. "Thank you."

He closed the door behind him.

I'd never been involved in a police investigation before. My only prior experience with the police was the one time I was speeding in high school and got pulled over—and that was just me getting a ticket. This was quite a bit different. I walked over to the window and looked out. My room faced the side yard, so I couldn't see the front of the house, or the back.

But that damned maze was there in sight, just to my left.

I shivered.

None of this made any sense.

Why would anyone kill Angus?

I shook my head. For all I knew, there were any number of people with a reason to want to kill Angus. I tried to remember what little I knew of him. I knew he was related to Maeve and several of the other people who worked on the estate—they were all McPhersons, one way or another.

I shivered again.

Other than whoever had killed him, I was the last person to see him alive.

That was…that was a bit much to handle.

The killer had probably been out there, watching and waiting, while I was speaking to Angus.

And Angus knew. Angus knew his killer was there, was going to kill him. He was trying to signal me, trying to get me out of there but somehow let me know something.

The answer is at the center of the maze.

What on earth did that mean? Maybe if I'd been a little less self-absorbed and paid a little more attention, he might be alive right now.

No, don't go there. It wasn't your fault.

But I still couldn't understand why anyone would kill Angus. Sure, he was a bit gruff and could be unfriendly. I'd seen him be borderline rude to Peggy before, but he was devoted to Sea Oats and to the Swann family. I remembered that his wife had died years earlier, and he didn't have any children. I couldn't wrap my mind around it being a crime of passion. But Angus's death, while shocking, also made me take stock of myself a bit more. I'd lived at Sea Oats for a year, and I knew next to nothing about him or any of the other staff on the estate, other than their names and some bits and pieces here and there.

I wasn't sure I liked what that said about me.

The only thing that made any sense to me was that it had to be some random thing, some trespasser on the grounds. Maybe someone who was mentally unbalanced? Angus was very protective of Sea Oats, had often run trespassers off with a rifle and threats. Maybe he'd gotten into a scuffle or something with his killer and it was an accident? Self-defense?

I walked out of my room and down the stairs, back to the library. Someone had cleared the tray—Maeve, no matter how rattled, always made sure things got taken care of—and I wondered if it would be in bad taste for me to go down to the kitchen for some coffee, and to see how Maeve was doing.

Probably.

I walked over into the tower section and looked out the windows. The ambulance, its lights off, was leaving, and there were now four police cars out there. The tour van was still parked where it had been.

Karen was going to have a hard time explaining this to her group, I thought as I sat down in one of the window seats. A drop of rain hit the window and the wind rattled the panes. The storm was about to break.

"What's going on?" a voice asked from the library door, startling me.

I got up and walked back into the library. A man I didn't recognize was standing in the doorway. He was about midforties, with a shaved head and strongly built body. He was wearing a tight black long-sleeved T-shirt that showed off his strong muscles and narrow waist. His black jeans were also tight, but incongruously he was wearing a pair of slippers. His face was a perfect oval, his eyes enormous and brown. A thick single eyebrow stretched across his lower forehead. He hadn't shaved today—there was salt-and-pepper stubble scattered over his face.

"And you are?" I asked. My voice sounded distant, far away. I shook my head and held out my hand, adding in a friendlier tone, "I'm Ariel Montgomery."

"The interior decorator?" The right side of the eyebrow went up, a smile creeping across the thick lips. "I saw that piece on you in the Sunday *Times* a few weeks ago. Nice to meet you." He took my hand and shook it. "I'm Dustin Rockwell."

The name was familiar to me, but I couldn't quite place it. "It was actually a couple of months ago, but thank you."

"What's with the cops?" he asked, ignoring what I'd said.

"Angus, the head groundskeeper, has been killed," I replied, shivering again.

"Killed?"

"Murdered. Someone hit him over the head with a shovel."

He goggled at me. "Who would kill a groundskeeper?"

"That," I said, turning and walking back to my chair, "is why the police were called."

He followed me into the room, sitting down in the chair recently occupied by Peggy. "Wow. I'm not sure how to wrap my mind around that, you know? I don't think I've ever been in a house where someone was killed before."

"It's a first for me, too."

"What are you doing here? Are you going to be redecorating the place?" He glanced around. "The place could use some sprucing up. It's like no one's redecorated since the place was built."

"I—" I stopped, and then figured there was no point in not telling him the truth. "I'm married to Charlotte Swann. We've been separated for almost two years."

"Oh, yes, of course, how stupid of me. I knew that." He wiped crumbs from his face. "Sorry, my mind is in the nineteenth century, and sometimes it takes me a while to return to the present. I'm writing a biography of Arabella Swann. Peggy's invited me here to stay while I work, and as a struggling author, I never turn down a free place to stay."

That was where I'd heard of him before. He'd made a name for himself as an expert on New York's upper crust in the nineteenth century. His book *The Commodore's Daughters*, about the daughters of Commodore Cornelius Vanderbilt, founder of the fabled American dynasty, had been on the best seller lists for nearly three years and had been adapted into a hugely successful miniseries on one of the pay cable networks.

The follow-up, *The Two Mrs. Asters*, was almost as successful as his first.

He was the perfect biographer for Arabella Swann, and it was past time for someone to write about her. I'd never read a book about her.

I was about to ask him another question when the cop showed up at the door, looking for Dustin. I excused myself to let them have the room and went downstairs. I couldn't imagine there were many murders in Penobscot; the most the cops here ever had to deal with most likely were drunk and out-of-control tourists, or bar fights.

I slipped down the back stairs. Maeve was in the kitchen, sitting at the table, staring at her hands when I came through the door.

"Are you okay?" I asked, touching her on the shoulder.

She touched my hand and nodded. "I'll be all right, Miss Ariel. It's just the shock, you know?"

"He was your...cousin, wasn't he?"

She smiled, wiping at her eyes again. "Yes, Angus is—was—my cousin. We weren't close—he was a difficult man, especially after Karla, his wife, died. I always thought that maybe if they'd had some children he might not have turned out the way he did. He was so closed off after she died, never went to church anymore, didn't want to have anything to do with anyone." She nodded. "He bit my head off a time or two when I suggested he do something social, or had a woman I wanted to set him up with. All he cared about was doing his job and that damned maze."

I repeated what he said to me. "Does that make any sense to you?"

She made a face and shook her head. "The only thing at the center of that maze is the map to get out"—she pushed her chair back from the table—"and everyone knows that."

I'd forgotten about the map. About fifteen years ago—I'm not sure when it was, but that sounded about right—a guest's child had gotten lost in the maze and couldn't find her way back out again from the center. Since the trick was to get to the center, it was decided that a map showing the easiest way to get back out again would be put in the center of the maze.

I would have had it pulled up by the roots, but that was just me.

"Do you want some coffee?" Maeve asked, getting down a can from one of the cupboards.

"I don't want to be any trouble…"

"I was going to make it anyway," Maeve replied with a slight shrug. "Keeping busy is the best thing for me to do." She smiled sadly. "I don't like to wallow, I like to work."

I sat there for a while and drank coffee with her for a few minutes, until she shooed me out so she could start getting to work on dinner.

I escaped back up the stairs. I was starting up the flight to the third floor when Peggy called my name.

"Oh, there you are." She looked tired and anxious. "Given the circumstances, I hope you don't mind too much, but I'm going to ask Maeve to just put out a buffet-style dinner in the dining room on the sideboard around six." She ran a hand through her hair. "It's just awful. I can't imagine…" She shivered. "Why on earth would anyone kill Angus?"

"It doesn't make any sense," I agreed, and went on up to my room.

I went down to dinner around seven, when I couldn't stand the hunger anymore. The dining room was empty, but there was a stack of dirty dishes and silverware in a gray plastic tub on a chair next to the sideboard. I made myself a thick ham sandwich and sat down at the table, wondering if anyone would come down.

No one did, so I wolfed it down and grabbed a bottle of wine from the kitchen to take back upstairs with me. I drank three glasses of wine while checking my email and social media accounts and was a bit woozy when I closed the laptop and put the cork back into the bottle. It was still raining, and the constant patter of rain against my windows, and the occasional blast of wind around the corner of the house, were kind of soothing. I put on the Chicago Bears football jersey I always slept in, and got under the covers. I switched off the light and stared at the ceiling.

It didn't surprise me that I had trouble falling asleep that night.

The bed in the green room was comfortable, of course, and the high-thread count Egyptian cotton sheets and velvet covers felt warm and soft. I'd forgotten, though, how cold it always seemed to be at Sea Oats. I don't know if it was the high ceilings or the fact the building was so old, but when the temperature dropped I never could get warm inside the house. The wind and rain were still whipping around the house, rattling the big windows, and I lay there for what seemed like hours, waiting to fall asleep. I would have thought the three glasses of wine would have helped, but my mind didn't want to shut down.

Seeing Charlotte again, Angus being killed...either would have been enough to make me sleepless; the combination of the two was enough to keep me awake through the weekend, probably.

Charlotte had looked...good. There had been that small part of me, the part I don't like to admit to anyone is there, that hoped she would look a wreck, like losing me had been such a horrible thing that it would show on her face, in her figure.

Terrible, I knew. Not one of the parts of my personality that I was proud of, but it was true.

She not only looked good, she looked *fantastic*, even better than I remembered. The additional gray in her hair was sexy, and she looked like she was in even better physical condition than when we'd been together. So many memories flashed through my head, like a crazy kaleidoscope. Her climbing out of the pool at the villa we'd rented in Panzano, Italy, for our honeymoon, the water droplets scattered over her trim, strong muscles, the rising of gooseflesh in the cool wind as she shook water from her hair. Her coming out of the shower in the hotel room in Venice where we'd gone next, standing in the window looking at the fireworks celebrating the Festival of the Redeemer, her arm around my waist, my head nestled into the space between her shoulder and her neck, smelling her clean skin, feeling her body heat. The way it felt having her warmth beside me in our bed every night, and how much I hated sleeping alone now…All of it making me realize I still loved her, I still wanted her, that I had made a horrible mistake in walking out of her life two years ago, that I had spent the last two years convincing myself I was happy and could get on with my life.

I'd been lying to myself the entire time.

And seeing her looking so good, so sexy, so beautiful, like she not only wasn't upset I'd left but had also *thrived* without me, was just another twist of the knife in my heart. Which also meant I was a terrible person. She looked like she hadn't even lost a night's sleep about me, and my biggest fear—that she was glad I was gone, had washed her hands of the whole mess, and moved on—was, apparently, the truth.

It wasn't the most mature attitude, and I wasn't sure I liked what it said about me as a person, but it was how I felt.

I shouldn't have run away. I should have stayed and fought for my marriage.

Now it was too late.

So, why was I staying? Why didn't I just take my suitcase and have Joseph drive me to the LIRR station, head back into the city to my life and my career, and forget about Sea Oats and Charlotte Swann?

Because...because I wasn't going to leave until and unless Charlotte asked me to.

The fact she hadn't filed for divorce had to count for something, right? No matter how angry she'd been two years ago, she still had to have some feelings for me, didn't she?

You always throw away happiness with both hands, my mother had said to me once, when I was a teenager, exasperated with whatever drama was going on in my life at the time. I couldn't even remember what it was, but I'd never forgotten my mother saying that to me. Sometimes I heard it in my sleep. Sometimes, when I was feeling emotional and needed to make a decision, I stopped and ask myself, *Are you throwing happiness away? Is that logical? Are you being irrational? Are you going to regret this?*

If I had stopped and asked myself that the night I ran away from Sea Oats, I might have stayed. And had I stayed, how differently would things have worked out?

God, what a fool I'd been.

I'd never stopped loving Charlotte. Sure, I pretended like I didn't care, that I was over it, but now that I'd seen her again? I couldn't pretend even to myself anymore.

I loved her. I still wanted her, desired her, wanted to feel her body next to mine in bed at night, wanted to feel her lips against mine, her firm breasts in my hands, our mouths on each other's bodies. I wanted to make up, I wanted her to tell me she loved me and wanted me back, I wanted everything the way it had once been.

I didn't want a divorce.

I didn't want to leave.

But it was too late now.

I sat up in the bed and brooded, pulling my knees up and wrapping my arms around them. Running away had made me look guilty, hadn't it? Of course Bast wasn't going to be honest about what happened, and Peggy was going to believe anything Bast said the way she always did, but Charlotte...that was what had hurt me the most. Sure, we hadn't been getting along. Sure, I was being childish about how busy she was with her work and that she wasn't spending enough time with me. If I'd been a little more mature, a little more adult, I would have seen that her job required a lot of her time and it wasn't personal. I should have gone back to work myself. I shouldn't have quit my job in the first place. Hollis herself had warned me, when I gave her my notice after our whirlwind three-month courtship and marriage. "You're going to need more than just being a wife," she'd said, but I'd not taken her words seriously. Hollis was devoted to her work to the exclusion of everything else; she was on her fourth husband and the rumor around the office was this marriage, barely two years old, was already in trouble, and she was talking to her lawyers. But she had been right. Part of the problem was I was bored, and instead of going back to work or finding something useful to do with my time...

No, there was no sense in rehashing all that again. The past couldn't be changed, only the future. And I needed to sit down and talk to Charlotte about everything, and put an end to the marriage.

I lay back down and closed my eyes, and drifted off into an odd half sleep, where I was kind of asleep and dreaming but also partially awake and aware. It wasn't restful, but my mind, my dreams, seemed particularly vivid.

I was outside the hedge maze, afraid to go inside but somehow, for some reason, I knew I had to, whether I wanted to or not. Old Angus was there suddenly, at my side, repeating those words over and over again in his hoarse whiskey-raw voice. *The answer's in the maze, the answer's in the maze*, and then a shadow fell over both of us. I was afraid and I ran to the entrance into the maze, and behind me I heard Angus cry out and there was a bone-crushing thud and I knew he'd just been murdered, and the killer was coming for me next. I ran into the maze and around a corner. The maze was tall enough to block out the sun and it was cold in there. Everything was in shadows so I could barely see. I moved quickly, because I could hear him coming, looking for me, calling my name.

Ariel...where are you, Ariel? You can't hide from me forever.

I was terrified, absolutely terrified, and I went around a corner and then—

A loud crash in the hallway woke me from the dream and I sat up straight in the bed, reaching for the switch on the lamp next to the bed.

I grabbed my robe and hurried to the door. I opened it, and the hallway was empty. But I could hear noise from downstairs. The grandfather clock in the hallway showed it was just after two.

Who was up at this hour downstairs?

And then I caught the faint smell of smoke.

I grabbed my tennis shoes and my jacket and headed for the back staircase. The smoke smell wasn't strong so I doubted the house was on fire, but it was still best to get down from the third floor just in case. As I reached the landing at the second floor I could hear more voices coming from downstairs— people were in the kitchen. I hurried down as fast as I could go and burst through the kitchen door. Peggy was pouring herself a cup of coffee, and a young woman I didn't know was sitting at the kitchen table.

"You just missed Charlotte," Peggy said, glancing at me as she sat down at the table. "Help yourself to coffee."

"I'm good. What's going on?" I sat down at the table.

"The shed is on fire," the other woman replied. She was in her nightgown, which left very little to the imagination, and she didn't look like she'd been asleep. "I'm Kayla." She narrowed her eyes curiously. "You must be Ariel."

"I am," I replied. Her frank way of staring at me was making me uncomfortable. She was beautiful in a strangely waifish way, with enormous eyes and a head that seemed almost too large for her slender body. She had long reddish-blond hair sloppily parted in the center, and she wasn't wearing any makeup. Her skin was incredible. Even in the late night kitchen lighting, it glowed. "Your *Vogue* cover was gorgeous."

"Thanks," she replied in her childish voice. She seemed younger than she must have been—but then she could have started as a young teen.

"What shed is on fire?"

"Charlotte's office," Peggy clarified tiredly. "The fire department is on their way, but I think it's under control."

"Arson," Kayla said.

"We don't know that, Kayla," Peggy said, her voice sharp. "Coffee, Ariel?"

I shook my head. "No, thanks. I just heard some commotion—but if it's under control, maybe I'll just try to go back to sleep."

"I'll come with you," Kayla said. She got up and tucked her arm through mine. "There's nothing going on around here."

She was taller than I was, but not by much. "Is Bast here?"

"No, he got hung up in the city and he'll be out tomorrow in the morning." She yawned. Her teeth were glistening white and as perfect as the rest of her. "I know all about what happened with you and Bast, you know."

We'd reached the first landing and my heart sank. "I—"

"I've heard his story, is what I mean." She cut me off with a wink and a smile. "Bast tells his own lies so often he starts believing they're true. He's convinced himself you threw yourself at him." When I started to splutter she cut me off again. "I'm sure it was all Bast, it almost always is, but he had to tell that lie to Charlotte and now he's told it so many times he believes it." She laughed. "I think part of the reason he loves me is because I see through his bullshit."

I didn't trust myself to answer. I was still angry with him—it wasn't entirely his fault, but I'd been stupid to trust him.

We reached the third floor and walked down the hallway to my door. "I'm on the other end." She impulsively hugged me. "I hope we're going to be friends."

"That would be nice," I replied and escaped into my room. I walked over to the window and looked out. Of course, I couldn't see anything.

I sat back down on the bed.

Charlotte thought someone had been searching through her office. Someone had killed Angus, and now her office had been set on fire.

What on earth was going on at Sea Oats?

CHAPTER FIVE

I fell back into that awful, restless half-sleep.

It was a horrible night of tossing and turning and waking up, it seemed, every half hour from this horrific nightmare that somehow managed to start over again each time I fell back into sleep, like the DVR in my brain hit pause every time I woke up and play every time my mind lapsed into the right stage of sleep. In the dream, I was inside the maze—that horrible, horrible green monstrosity—and someone was after me, trying to kill me, and I couldn't find my way out. The hedge seemed alive, the branches and leaves reaching for me, trying to twist around my wrists and ankles and drag me down, and magically I seemed to sometimes have a machete to cut myself free, but I had to be quiet and careful so the person who was after me wouldn't find me, but I could hear him, his heavy breathing, calling for me, *Ariel...Ariel...why are you hiding from me Ariel come out come out from wherever you are Ariel you can't hide from me forever come out Ariel...*

I sat up in bed with a start, my heart racing and my hands shaking, in a cold sweat. At first I didn't know where I was, lost and disoriented, just aware that I wasn't in my bed, my apartment, panting as the adrenaline from the nightmare faded away, leaving me shaking slightly.

I shook my head, trying to shake the cobwebs and the last vestiges of the horror from my mind.

Someone knocked on the door, and I remembered finally that I was at Sea Oats.

"Just a moment," I called, reaching for my robe as I slid out of bed. My hair was slightly damp, and I glanced at the time on my phone. It was just before nine, and I ran fingers through my hair in a desperate attempt to look, if not presentable, then human at least.

"Miss Ariel, it's Maeve. Miss Peggy thought you might prefer having breakfast in your room this morning, rather than coming down."

Peggy was still, apparently, very thoughtful. It was part of the reason I'd believed she was my friend back when I lived here.

I opened the door. "Thank you, Maeve—be sure to thank Peggy for me."

Maeve's eyes were red and swollen, and her hair was loose and down, rather than pulled back into the sensible bun she usually sported. I started to take the silver serving tray from her but she shifted slightly with a shake of her head. "If you want to get back into bed, I can set it up for you."

Defeated, I stepped aside so she could enter. "You can just put it on the desk," I said. "I haven't even had time to wash my face so…" I watched as she set the tray down. The coffee smelled heavenly, and my stomach growled. Maeve was an amazing cook. I'd have to be careful or I'd regain the ten pounds I'd finally lost after leaving Sea Oats. "Are you all right? Shouldn't you have stayed home from work today?"

She shook her head. "Work is the best thing for me, Miss Ariel," she replied. "If I stayed home all I would do is wallow, and that never comes to a good end, I find." She nodded. "Keeping busy—that way I don't have time to stop and feel bad." She hesitated, and her eyes filled with tears. "I just...I just don't know who would want to do such a thing. Angus was difficult, sure, but not so that someone would kill him. It just doesn't make any sense to me." She wiped her eyes with the corner of her apron. "My apologies, Miss Ariel. My troubles aren't yours."

"If there's anything I can do—"

She shook her head and slipped out the door.

I felt useless.

I'd never understood, or liked, or been comfortable with, the separation between the servers and the served at Sea Oats. I hadn't grown up with servants, obviously, and I thought I hadn't gotten used to it. But now, with Maeve clearly grieving for her cousin, I wasn't sure what was the right thing to do. Should I have hugged her, or would that have been crossing some line I didn't know or understand? I couldn't believe Peggy had allowed her to come to work.

On the other hand, Peggy had known her for years, so she probably knew better than I did. Still, it seemed almost inhuman in a way.

Marrying Charlotte, I reflected as I walked into the bathroom, had been an enormous mistake. I didn't belong at a place like Sea Oats. I had more in common with the staff than I did with the family. I'd grown up in the Midwest, in suburban Kansas. My mother would have laughed at the idea of anyone else cleaning her house or cooking for her family. My first job had been waiting tables when I was sixteen, and I'd waited tables all the way through college. I'd never gotten used to the idea of having staff, of acting like they didn't exist, talking about personal things like they weren't there. Maeve didn't work weekends, but she was always at the house from early in the morning on Monday till late, every night. She oversaw the cleaning crew from the service that came in three days a week, she cooked all the meals, did all the shopping, and the house ran like a clock.

For twelve months, the woman had cooked my meals, made sure my clothes were laundered, had picked up after me and never complained, never had a cross expression on her face—and I didn't know if she was married, had children, anything personal about her.

I didn't even know how old she was.

The only personal things I knew about her—like she was related to Angus and some of the other groundskeepers—I'd picked up from things members of the family had said or conversations I'd overheard between her and them.

Was this the kind of person I wanted to be, spoiled and unconcerned about the staff, thinking of them only in terms of how they could make my life easier, how well they waited on me?

No, it wasn't.

I'd been uncomfortable with the staff when I'd come here to live, not sure how to talk to them or how to address them, and I'd disliked giving them orders. Peggy had a natural gift for dealing with the staff, effortlessly giving orders in a light, pleasant way that made them seem like suggestions more than anything else. Charlotte was the same—even Bast managed to make orders sound like a request. Even after a year, I'd not quite managed to get past my discomfort. I'd been raised to clean up after myself, and it was strange to leave dirty dishes on the table or to not make my own bed or do my own laundry. I'd always liked doing those things, once I got past my resentment about my mother making me do them. I'd used to think how lovely it would be to have people to do that for me. But the reality wasn't quite what I'd expected.

It so rarely was.

I went back into the bedroom and arranged myself and the tray on the bed. I removed the plate cover—crispy bacon, buttered toast and strawberry jam, one egg scrambled dry. All my favorites—Maeve hadn't forgotten, even after two years.

I blinked back some tears.

I poured the coffee and started eating. It was, of course, perfect. I checked my email on my phone while I ate, and deleted all the junk. There wasn't anything that needed immediate attention, thank God. I had another cup of coffee. When there was nothing left but crumbs I put the tray outside my door—something else that had taken me a long time to get used to, the way you just could put things out in the hall and someone would take care of it, like in a hotel.

I'll take it down to the kitchen myself after I shower, I decided, closing the door behind me. It wasn't like Maeve was hovering in the hall, anyway, waiting for me to finish. I smiled to myself as I started the shower and picked out something to wear.

I might be staying at Sea Oats, but I wasn't going to go back to depending on the staff waiting on me hand and foot. It was my little way of rebelling, rejecting the Swann lifestyle.

As I showered, I thought about my conversation with Angus and the nightmare I'd had again. *The secret is in the center of the maze.* What the hell did he mean by that?

The police didn't seem to think it had anything to do with him being killed, and maybe it didn't.

It still creeped me out that I was the last person to see him alive. I couldn't help thinking he'd been trying to tell me something.

Maybe he was trying to ask me for help.

That was a horrible thought.

If so, he'd been asking the wrong person.

I picked up the tray and carried it down the back stairs to the kitchen. Maeve was doing the dishes when I backed through the swinging door with the tray.

"Miss Ariel, you should have called me! I would have brought that down." She dried her hands on a towel before taking the tray from me.

I felt scolded. "You have enough to do around here as it is," I replied, and I felt a guilty blush spread up my neck, "and I didn't want to bother you. I can carry a tray down myself, you know." I poured myself another cup of coffee from the pot on the counter and sat down at the kitchen table. I knew she was going to say it wasn't a bother before she said it, and so I just nodded in response. "Is everyone else up?"

"Miss Charlotte went into the city," she said as she started placing my dirty dishes into the soapy water. "Miss Kayla doesn't usually get up before noon, if then. Miss Peggy went into town to talk to that Karen Wilson woman about canceling the tours for the next few days." She pursed her lips. Her tone made it clear she didn't approve of either Karen Wilson or the tours. "And if you'll pardon me saying it," she'd lowered her voice, "I wish they'd cancel them for good."

"Get a cup of coffee and take a break," I replied with a smile. I'd known Maeve wouldn't like the tours.

"Don't mind if I do." Maeve got herself a cup of coffee and joined me at the table. She gave me one of her biggest smiles. "It's so nice having you back in the house, Miss Ariel. I hope you're here to stay."

"Oh, thank you, Maeve, but I don't know how long I'll be staying. I have to be back at work next Monday. What is up with the tours, anyway? I was surprised when I saw the flyer at the inn."

"And weren't you sly, to come back here on the tour." Maeve winked at me over the rim of her coffee cup.

I cringed inwardly at being caught out. "Yes, well...I didn't know how I'd be received."

"Well." She gave me a look. "Do you mind if I speak plainly?"

"Of course not." I hated that she even had to ask. "You can always speak your mind with me, Maeve. I'm not really a member of the family anymore, anyway."

"Now stop that." She wagged her finger at me. "You're a Swann whether you like it or not, Miss Ariel."

"And you don't have to call me Miss, either."

She barked out a laugh, and her brown eyes sparkled. "That's a habit I don't want to get out of. I know my place here, Miss Ariel. The Swanns have been very good to me and my family over the years. Miss Charlotte paid for my kids to go to college, every penny." She preened. "All three of my boys have degrees, thanks to her. I'm very grateful." She leaned across the table. "I may be talking out of turn here, but Miss Charlotte has never been the same since you left." She tutted. "And weren't you a bad girl for running away like you did! Running away from problems is never the answer, Miss Ariel."

"I know." I got up and refilled my cup. I was going to be bouncing off the walls soon at this rate. "But I'm here now. Do you think Charlotte...do you think she wants me to go?"

"I can't speak for her." She shrugged. "But she's had a lot on her plate lately, and I think she's glad you're home."

Home. I'd never thought of Sea Oats as home when I lived here.

"So, what exactly is going on around here, Maeve?" I asked as I sat back down, watching her face. Maeve knew everything that went on at Sea Oats.

She pursed her lips.

"I never said thank you for how good you were to me

when Charlotte brought me here," I said, and I meant it. "I owe you so much for making me feel welcome."

"Oh, Miss Ariel." Her voice softened. "It was my pleasure. You made Miss Charlotte so happy. She was never that happy when she was—" She broke off.

I knew what she was going to say though.

She was never that happy when she was with Lindsay Moore.

Maeve liked Lindsay even less than Peggy did, which was saying something.

"Isn't she seeing Lindsay Moore again?"

Maeve's face was expressionless. "A few dinner dates don't mean anything. They've known each other all their lives." She met my eyes. "You're the one she loves, Miss Ariel."

I doubted that, but it was nice to hear.

"As for the others"—she took another sip of her coffee— "there's some trouble, all right. I don't know what it all means, or what all is going on, but I…I hear things."

"I won't tell anyone you said a word."

"Well," she whispered, glancing back and forth, "there's some trouble with Mr. Sebastian."

Her tone made it clear she disapproved. She'd told me once that he'd been spoiled and that was his trouble. "He needed his behind paddled a lot more than he got." Bast himself had told me that she'd never forgiven him for all the pranks he'd pulled on her when he was a kid.

"What else is new?" I rolled my eyes, hoping she'd elaborate. "Isn't he always in some kind of trouble?"

"He does seem to attract trouble, doesn't he?" She tutted. "Maybe if he would get a job and do some hard work, like a man, he'd grow up and stop giving Miss Charlotte and Miss Peggy gray hair. They've always spoiled that boy."

"He's not a boy anymore, Maeve."

"Then he needs to stop acting like one!" She shook her head. "And do some growing up!"

"What is it this time?"

"Money, what else? It's always money, isn't it?" She sighed. "You know he always feels he has to compete with Miss Charlotte. But he's risked too much this time." She sighed again. "I don't understand how it all works, but he borrowed a lot of money to invest in some business and used his shares of the company as collateral, and now he has to pay it back and he doesn't have the money, so I know Miss Charlotte is at her wits' end trying to come up with the money for him."

That was par for the course. Char had been bailing Bast out of trouble his entire life.

"Is it true that someone is targeting the company?"

"Miss Charlotte says so, and she would know. I know she also thinks someone has been breaking into her office." Maeve shrugged. "She's hired security for the house, what with the fire last night and"—her voice broke—"what happened to Angus yesterday."

"Oh, Maeve." I reached across the table and took one of her hands. "I'm sorry—I didn't want to upset you."

"You haven't upset me." She blew out a breath. "Angus is gone, no amount of blubbering or feeling sorry for myself is going to change that."

"Had Angus—well, had he been himself lately?"

She made a face. "Same as always, ornery and a pain in my behind." She smiled faintly. "Always slipping in here and tasting what I'm cooking, never a kind word for anyone, but you know he was always teasing, there wasn't a mean bone in his body. And he'd have died for the Swanns." Her hand flew up to her mouth. "Oh."

"When I saw him yesterday—before it happened—he told

me something weird," I said slowly. "He told me the secret was in the center of the maze. Do you know what he meant by that?"

"That damned maze." She got up and put our cups in the sink. "No, I don't know what he meant by that. He was crazy about that stupid maze." She tapped her fingers on the counter for a moment. "Maybe he meant something about Mr. Bast."

"Bast?"

"You know when Mr. Bast was a boy he played a trick on Angus, with the maze." She looked pensive. "He dug up one of the bushes and left it in the center of the maze. Angus was fit to be tied. Of course, Mr. Bast never got punished for it."

Her tone clearly added, *He never got punished for anything.*

"Thanks, Maeve." I stood up. "I think I'm going to go for a walk."

She glanced out the window. "You'd best hurry—it's going to rain again."

It was still gray and damp outside, and there were beads of water on the grass. The ground looked soft and wet, and I was glad for the paved walks as I headed along the path that led past the front of the maze and to Charlotte's office. I wasn't sure why I wanted to see it—that impulse that causes drivers to slow down and stare at accidents, maybe—but I wanted to take a look.

When we were married, Charlotte had spent a good fifty percent of her time at Sea Oats in her office. I used to join her sometimes, sit in a chair with a book while she read reports and answered emails. I never felt comfortable in her office; it was typical Charlotte, really. Charlotte didn't care about interior design, whether furniture matched or any of the details of how to make her office comfortable and homey. She honestly believed interior design was a waste of time, which was kind of a problem for me since it was my training and my career. Since it wasn't a real skill to her, my having to give up my career to marry her and live at Sea Oats wasn't a problem. Not having your life's work, your interests, taken seriously by the person you marry wasn't a good thing. It made me feel discounted, unimportant, seen as lesser.

We were not a good match.

I didn't like the person I became while living here, and now that I was back, I could see that leaving was the best thing I could have done. No matter how I felt about Charlotte, I should have never married her. It was too fast after we started seeing each other, and we were both so caught up in the magic and passion and novelty of being in love we didn't stop to think about what being married would mean, about who we were and how we could integrate each other into our separate lives.

I'd been unfair to Charlotte, too. I'd let all my insecurities and problems and issues bubble under the surface, never saying anything, not wanting to create more stress for her than running an international company already did. She was often tired and strung out when she finally made it home in the evenings and I didn't want to add to her burden. So instead of talking to her I tried to keep my boredom from her, my loneliness, and tried to entertain myself in other ways.

Hardly the recipe for a successful marriage.

The maze loomed over me as I walked alongside it. It sheltered me from the cold wind blowing off the ocean, and the sun was hidden behind gray and black and white clouds. The air felt wet, like it was heavy with rain and just waiting for the chance to start. The dirt in the flower beds was that dark wet black that meant saturation, which wouldn't be good for the flowers, and I couldn't help but wonder about the maze. Angus was head groundskeeper but had any number of helpers to work on the grounds so he could primarily focus on the hedge maze. Who would do it now that he was dead?

If it were up to me the hedges would all be pulled up by the roots and burned.

Well, maybe trimmed down a bit, I thought. I stopped and looked at the hedge. There was no way any Swann would agree to get rid of the hedge since it had been put in as one of Arabella's whims. As I stared at its green impenetrability, I thought about Arabella. When I'd lived here, I'd been fascinated by her. She'd been a woman ahead of her time, a spoiled and indulged only child, heiress to a shipping fortune. Her parents actually had hoped to marry her off to a bankrupt European nobleman, but Arabella had confounded everyone by falling in love with and marrying Samuel Swann, a widower with no children who was some twenty-five years her senior. She'd been an ardent feminist at a time when such a thing was unheard of, let alone in the aristocratic circles she traveled in. I was glad someone was finally writing her biography—it was long overdue. Most of the family stories about Arabella were probably myth, embellished and embroidered over many retellings since she'd died. Samuel had the maze planted for her, the bushes imported from England to replicate the one she'd been so fascinated by on that long-ago English country estate. There hadn't been anything like it anywhere else in North America, and so it had been a bit of a wonder, still was, in fact.

The wind shifted a bit and I could smell stale smoke, so I started walking again. Charlotte's office, the dower house Samuel had built so Arabella's mother could have her own home, was a small Tudor-style building. I'd often wondered how Arabella's mother had adapted to living in such a small place—the story was she'd moved in there after it was finished and she'd never lived in the city mansion and never visited the place in Newport. I'd always kind of doubted that story; it hardly seemed realistic that a wealthy widow would so drastically cut back her lifestyle once her husband had died. It seemed like a kind of quaint notion from the Victorian era that a widow had to shut herself up away from the world and wait for death.

I rounded the corner of the maze and gasped at the sight of the cottage. I'd always thought it was kind of a cute place. Before Charlotte turned it into a workspace for herself it had been used primarily as a guest house after the death of its original occupant. The downstairs was all one enormous room, with a fireplace at either end, with a small galley kitchen tucked into a corner opposite the hanging staircase that led upstairs to the two bedrooms and the bathroom. There was a third bedroom in the attic, but it was primarily used now for storage.

The entire front of the building was blackened and windows had been broken out. The scorch marks ran along the upper floors, and the flowers in the beds in front were burned to a crisp. The grass was also scorched, and the front door was open. I could hear faint voices, and as I approached, a man in a suit came outside, talking to Charlotte. They shook hands and he gave me a look as he took the walk that led the other way, around Sea Oats and to the driveway.

My heart leaped when I saw her, and I felt an involuntary smile form. My eyes went from her face down her figure and back up again.

A chance to speak to her alone, maybe get the conversation started, see if there was a chance…

I started walking toward her.

Of course Charlotte scowled when she saw me coming her way.

"Lovely to see you, too, good morning," I said, my smile

fading as I approached. She was wearing a navy blue pantsuit, and she looked tired. "Were you able to get any sleep last night?"

"A little." She ran her left hand through her hair, which fell back into place neatly. She exhaled. "This is the worst possible time for you to be here, Ariel. Why did you come?"

I bit my lower lip. *Don't let her get under your skin.* "Don't you think we've been avoiding each other long enough?" I asked quietly, still covering for Peggy. Why Peggy didn't want Char to know she'd invited me was a mystery to me, but I didn't see any reason for me to say anything about it just yet.

"Just pack your things and go back into the city," Char said. "Joseph can drive you."

I felt myself getting angry. "Sea Oats is technically still my home," I replied hotly. "And in case you've forgotten, the police have told me I have to stay. I can move back into the inn if having me under the same roof is too much for you to bear."

I turned on my heel and started walking away quickly as angry tears formed in my eyes. I wiped them away and raised my chin defiantly as I kept walking, even though she called after me. I would be damned if I was ever going to let Charlotte Swann see me cry again. I walked back along the path the same way the insurance inspector had gone. Of course, she didn't follow me. Why should this time be any different?

I took a deep breath as I went around the corner of the house and caught my breath. The pond spread out to the left of the house and I could feel tears forming in my eyes again. It was calm, the surface slightly rippled by the wind, the dark water reflecting the gray clouds in the sky. A family of ducks was paddling happily along near the shoreline. I watched them, a faint smile on my face as I remembered the first time I'd ever seen the pond, when Charlotte had brought me here to meet the family and see the place.

I was so lost in memory I almost jumped out of my skin when someone called my name.

"Oh, I didn't mean to startle you," Roger Stanhope said, as he came down the side steps from the gallery, his arms spread wide.

"Roger!" I allowed him to give me one of his wonderful hugs and a kiss on the cheek. I'd always liked him. He'd always been nice to me, tutoring me on the sly about table settings and what fork was for what when I'd first come to Sea Oats as a socially awkward bride, worried about making a fool out of myself every time I turned around. "I understand congratulations are in order? How wonderful! I'm so happy for you."

"Oh, thank you, dear. Let me get a good look at you." He stepped back, his hands still on my arms, and scrutinized my face. "Let me guess, you've run into Charlotte, haven't you?"

"You always knew me too well, Roger." Roger was a handsome man who looked younger than he was. He had to be in his later fifties, but you'd never know it to look at him. Sure, there were some lines in his tanned face, but his brown eyes still sparkled with energy and youth. He was tall, maybe just over six feet, and he'd always been trim and fit. I suspect he colored his hair—the absence of any gray at his age couldn't have been natural. He was unseasonably tanned, and the arm he gave me was strong and tight. "You're so tan," I said as we climbed the stairs to the front gallery.

"I just got back from St. Bart's," he said, leading me to two wicker rocking chairs facing the pond. "Sit me with me a bit and let's catch up." Ever the gentleman, he waited for me to sit before sitting himself. He gestured with his head. "Still no swans out there."

I smiled faintly, even as his words tugged at my heart.

The story about the pond was one of those family legends

passed down through the generations—no one was sure if it was a true story or not anymore, but it was fun to think it was. Charlotte had told me the story on my first visit here.

Apparently, so the story went, when Samuel was looking for a place to build Arabella a summer home on Long Island, he'd never been satisfied with any of the land parcels he'd been shown. Getting tired of his dickering and dithering, Arabella came with him out to Penobscot to look at the land that eventually became Sea Oats. A family of swans had been paddling about on the pond, and she'd turned to Samuel and said, "Was there ever a better sign of where Swanns belong than this?" The great irony was the family of swans disappeared, driven away by the noise of the building the house and outbuildings and gardens. Even more strangely, swans were rarely seen on the pond. They'd become such a rarity that when a swan was spotted on the pond, people thought it was a sign of good fortune.

I'd always wondered if the swan on the pond when Charlotte had first brought me here was the real reason she'd married me. She'd been so excited to see a white swan out there on the water that day...

The wicker chair felt a little damp through my jeans. Oh, well, too late now. "Have you and Peggy been seeing each other long, Roger? I had no idea."

He smiled at me kindly. "It was one of those things, I suppose." He stared out over the lawn. "We'd known each other so long, then one morning we just realized we'd been right under each other's noses for so long. I do love her very much, you know. I didn't think I'd ever be able to, you know, love again, after Cathy died. This isn't a grand passion, of course—we're both too old for that sort of thing—but it's nice."

"I imagine Peggy will be happy to move out of here," I observed. "Your house will be a lot less for her to handle."

He laughed. "Did you really think Peggy would leave Sea Oats? No, my dear, we'll be living here."

"Oh, yes, of course." Peggy might be getting married, but obligations to Bast and Charlotte and Sea Oats would always come first with her. Roger apparently didn't have a problem with it.

"Now, tell me what you're doing here? I was surprised to hear you'd turned up. A pleasant surprise, to be sure, but still..." He rubbed his chin. He patted my leg. "I suppose I owe you an apology. I'm so sorry I didn't—" He hesitated. "I should have stayed in touch when you went back to the city."

"I could have reached out, too," I replied. "So I owe you an apology, too, Roger. I did think about you these past few years, though. It was—it just seemed...awkward, I suppose."

"No need to apologize to me, my dear. Let's just call it even and move forward, shall we?" He smiled at me. "So, what brings you back to Sea Oats after all this time?"

So Peggy hadn't told him she'd invited me, either. Interesting. "Closure, I guess, Roger. Kind of hard to go on with my life while I haven't dealt with my marriage." I made a feeble gesture. "I didn't know what I'd find when I got here, but it's pretty clear to me Charlotte's moved on."

"But what about you, Ariel? Have you moved on?"

I looked at his kind face. "Not yet." I shrugged. "There was a part of me that kept hoping, but..." I let my voice trail off.

"So you've heard the rumors about her and Lindsay, then?"

"Rumors?"

"They've had dinner a few times, Ariel. It's nothing to

worry about. They're old friends. Anything romantic died between them years ago."

Tell that to Lindsay, I thought, but aloud said, "It doesn't matter, Roger."

"If you still love her, then fight for her," Roger replied, grasping my hand. "I know she still has feelings for you, Ariel." He squeezed my hand tightly. "You know Charlotte is trying to fight a takeover of Swann's, right? Lindsay controls about two percent of the Swann's stock."

"So, you think—"

"I think you should stay and fight."

Chapter Six

I wanted desperately to believe him, even as I knew how pathetic my hopes were.

"I never believed that stupid story about you and Bast," he went on. "No one did." He made a face, and laughed. "Peggy did, of course. As you know, Bast can do no wrong in her eyes, and of course he's so good looking and wonderful and charming he can convert a lesbian."

I laughed. "Well, Peggy wasn't the only one who believed him. Charlotte believed it, too. I wouldn't have left if—if my wife hadn't believed I would not only cheat, but with a man, and her brother, no less." I shook my head, as the old feelings of bitterness and anger and hurt threatened to roil their way back up to the surface. I pushed them down and closed the door behind them, locking it for good measure. "I don't know. Maybe I shouldn't have run away. Maybe I should have stayed and fought, let the anger and hurt run their course and dealt with it. But Roger, I honestly didn't see another option back then, I didn't. Maybe I should have ridden out the storm. But"—I paused—"there's no point in rehashing it all. What's done is done. My marriage is over, and I know that now. So I guess the trip here wasn't in vain, at any rate."

"You're giving up," Roger said softly. "Don't give up so

easily, Ariel. I know you still love her—I can see it in your face. Don't give up without a fight. You'll regret it for the rest of your life."

"Maybe."

"Isn't it awful about old Angus?" He changed the subject, probably because of the look on my face. "Peggy said you were the last person to see him before—before it happened."

That was a jolt back into the present. "I know. So terrible. I mean, who would want to kill poor Angus? Have you heard anything from the police?"

He shook his head. "No, I'm afraid I don't know any more than anyone else. You didn't see anything or anyone, did you?"

"No." I shivered. "It kind of gives me the creeps knowing how close I was to the killer. But I didn't see anything."

He patted my leg. "I can't blame you for wanting to leave as soon as you can. But I really do think you should give things with Charlotte another chance. Don't leave without sitting down and having a good talk with her. Promise me that?"

"Yes, well." I got up and brushed his cheek with my lips. "I know you're coming from a good place, Roger, and it means a lot to me." I smiled at him. "You were always so nice to me, and I appreciate it more than you'll ever know. But if you'll excuse me, I didn't sleep very well last night and I think I'm going to go lie down for a bit."

"Of course." He smiled back at me. "It's really good to see you again, Ariel."

I walked around the corner of the house to the front. I managed to slip inside the front door before my eyes filled with tears again and I felt overwhelmed. Of course, it was easy for Roger to think it was possible for Charlotte and me to reconcile—he was happily engaged, had found love again at a time of his life when he probably thought it would never happen again for him. I was happy for him, and Peggy, but that didn't mean everything was going to work out okay for everyone else.

Hell, when Charlotte and I were happy, I'd wanted everyone else to be as happy as we were. But that was a long time ago. The reality now was different. I didn't belong here at Sea Oats anymore.

No, the sooner I could pack and get back to the city, the better off I would be.

I leaned back against the door, getting a hold of myself. The entryway was deserted, but I could hear a vacuum running somewhere on the first floor. I stood there for a moment, letting my façade slip a bit while I took a few deep breaths, his words still echoing inside my head.

I wished he was right, that I should stay and fight for Charlotte, but the simple truth I had to face and accept was that there was nothing left to fight for, even if I wanted to, even if I believed there was the slightest chance for me, for us. Charlotte had made it very clear she didn't love me anymore. Maybe he was right and she wasn't interested in Lindsay again, maybe the dinners were business related and Charlotte was just trying to make sure she had Lindsay's support in the stock fight at Swann's. Lindsay was the type to hold that over Charlotte's head, too.

That wasn't fair. I'd never liked Lindsay—she certainly had never given me any reason to like her—but was she the kind of woman who would blackmail Charlotte? Charlotte would never put up with anything like that, and would certainly never forgive her for it. She might need Lindsay's votes now, but once she didn't…Lindsay might be many things, but she wasn't a fool. She'd known Charlotte her entire life, and had made plenty of mistakes along the way. If she was smart—and she was—she would be supportive of Charlotte now for the dividends it would pay later.

It was hard for me to accept that Charlotte and Lindsay might get back together.

When we were happy together, Charlotte had told me that she'd stopped having deeper feelings for Lindsay years ago, that I had no reason to be jealous. Lindsay wasn't a threat. She'd told me about how deeply she'd been hurt when Lindsay had gotten married the first time. "I knew then she didn't love me," Charlotte had said, and I could hear the pain in her voice. "Besides, I never felt for her the way I do about you." She'd kissed me on the top of my head then, and we'd gone to bed.

No one had ever made me feel the way Charlotte could, either. She was an amazing lover, passionate yet patient, urgent but gentle. I'd tried not to remember that, tried not to think about the passionate nights in her arms, the feel of her lips against my body, the feel of her fingertips brushing my nipples, the way she could use her fingers and mouth to take me to heights I'd never dreamed were even possible, the way her skin felt against mine, the strong muscles in her arms and back…How I'd longed just to lie beside her in bed again, the warmth from her body comforting.

And now, being back here, I could admit to myself what I'd been in denial about for so long. The reason I hadn't dated, the reason I'd focused so much on work, was because I believed—*knew*—I'd never feel about another woman the way I did about Charlotte.

And no other woman could make me feel the way she did.

Why she hadn't filed for divorce remained a mystery to me. No matter how she felt for Lindsay now, it was clear she wasn't in love with me anymore. Maybe she'd just been waiting for me to file, I wasn't sure. More likely it was a pesky detail she didn't want to be bothered with and kept putting off. Divorce would be admitting failure, and if I knew anything about my wife, it was that she hated to fail at anything.

Even if she failed at this stock fight, she wouldn't give up. If she lost control of Swann's, she wouldn't rest until she was back in charge.

Peggy had told me once that Charlotte had always been obstinate.

I laughed to myself. Yes, that's a great reason to stay married! Not wanting to admit you'd failed at something.

I made up my mind. As soon as I was back in the city I was going to hire a lawyer and start the long, arduous process of untangling myself from the Swann family legally.

I put my hand against the door to keep my balance. That surge of emotion was unexpected. Where had that come from?

You always held out hope, that's where it came from, and now you know there isn't any. It's over. And it's okay to finally mourn for your marriage. You've been in denial for a long time, Ariel.

I took a deep breath.

If I was going to have a good cry, I wasn't going to do it down here.

The vacuum stopped, and I could hear idle chitchat among the female cleaning crew. The house was too much for Maeve to keep clean by herself, so three times a week a team of cleaners from town came out to clean the house thoroughly, from top to bottom. I walked over to the foot of the stairs, ready to head up to my room when I heard one of them say Angus's name.

One of the others shushed the speaker, and I crept down the hallway. The cleaning women were in the ladies' drawing room, and the door was open.

"Do you want Maeve to hear you?" one of them said in a thick Long Island accent, her voice hushed. "I don't know about you, but I need this job."

"You know as well as I do, Connie, there's been some

strange things going on around this place, and there has been for a while," the original speaker replied, her voice lower but still audible to me in the hallway. I glanced down the hall at the closed kitchen door. "I heard that old Angus had a lot of dirt on the Swann family, stuff they wouldn't want anyone to know, you know. And now that Miss Charlotte's *wife*"—the contempt positively dripped from the word—"is back, there's no telling what other kinds of perversions they're going to get up to around here."

"You think Charlotte Swann killed Angus?"

I didn't wait to hear the reply. I walked as quickly as I could to the stairs and then ran up them, taking them two at a time.

Charlotte? Was it possible that Charlotte could have—

She couldn't have. Charlotte would never—

You never thought she would believe you could have an affair with her brother, either.

How well do you really know your wife? How far would she go to keep control of Swann's?

I was being overdramatic. Sure, Charlotte had a temper—who didn't? But she would never kill anyone.

The fact that I was still alive was proof of that.

By the time I reached the third floor I was nearly out of breath and my leg muscles ached. I needed to lie down, get some more rest, stop thinking about murder and marriage and everything else that had my heart thumping.

I'd just managed to lie down on my bed and reach for my laptop when someone rapped on the door.

"May I come in?" Peggy asked, poking her head inside. "I don't want to disturb you."

"Of course, Peggy." I sat up better, propping the pillows behind me, gesturing for her to come in with a smile.

She sat down on the foot of the bed. "I wanted to thank you," she said, glancing back at the open door and lowering her voice, "for not telling Charlotte I'd asked you to come. I was terrified you'd tell her."

Terrified? I assumed she was exaggerating. I gave her a wan smile. "Yes, well, why get you in trouble?"

"Charlotte hates when I"—she made a face—"*interfere* in her life." She made air quotes when she said *interfere.* "She's made me swear I wouldn't do it again."

"You meant well," I replied.

"Yes, well, the path to hell and all that."

"How serious do you think the police were about me having to stay?"

"You want to leave?" She seemed surprised.

I reached for her hand and took it in both of mine. "Peggy, I appreciate you bringing me out here, don't get me wrong, and everything you thought you were doing came from a place of good, I know. But being back here"—I gestured around the room—"seeing Charlotte again…well, I don't know what you were hoping for, but it hasn't happened, nor will it. Charlotte and I—well, we are over. We have been for a long time." As I said the words I worried my eyes would get teary again, that my voice would crack with emotion.

Neither thing happened.

Maybe it was acceptance?

"Don't go, please. Stay another few days." Peggy got up and walked over to the window, opened the curtains and looked out. "There are some other things going on right now, distracting Charlotte. I know she still loves you, Ariel." She sighed. "I wish you would have called or emailed me before coming out here."

"But I—" I stopped. Time to get to the bottom of this

once and for all. "I did, Peggy, I told you yesterday. You never replied. That's why I did come now. You made it seem so urgent, so important. Was it not?"

"No, you and Charlotte need to get things settled, and I do still believe that needs to happen sooner than later." She turned back to me. "But when I emailed you, I didn't realize…I didn't know how bad things were going to get." She sighed. "Right now, well, Charlotte doesn't need this kind of distraction with everything else that's going on. And now with poor Angus…" Her voice broke.

"Do you think Angus's death has something to do with the takeover attempt?"

"I don't know. But Charlotte needs to focus on saving Swann's right now, and she doesn't need the distraction."

"Then I should go," I replied.

"No, no, don't." She wrung her hands. "That would just make it worse. It just never even crossed my mind you'd just come here. I thought, you know, we'd correspond or talk, and then, when the time was right, you'd come."

"As usual, I screwed up everything." I rolled my eyes. "I'm sorry, Peggy, but you have to understand—Charlotte is done with me. I appreciate your trying, though. It means a lot to me."

"I emailed you because Charlotte really seemed to need you. But things have changed, even in just the few days since I sent that email on impulse. But even so, please, don't go." She shook her head. "It doesn't matter now. You're here, so I'm asking you to be patient with her, okay? Can you wait a few more days before going back to the city?"

"You're not making a lot of sense. Tell me what's going on, Peggy."

"A few days more, Ariel. That's all I ask." She walked over to the door.

"Peggy—?"

"Be patient and everything will work out, you have to believe." She shut the door behind her.

I picked up one of the throw pillows and flung it at the door as hard as I could in frustration.

I was sorely tempted to just pack up and go—the police and the Swanns be damned.

The Swann family were some of the most aggravating people on the planet.

I couldn't wait for the day when I wasn't one of them anymore.

Resigned, I opened my laptop and started checking my emails, answering the ones from clients that couldn't wait until I was back in the city, deleting spam, and then an email from a potential client with a big country estate in Westchester triggered the memory of the pictures I'd taken on the grounds yesterday, before—before everything happened. The patterns on the lawn might be something they'd like as a color palette for that enormous living room with the big picture windows. I grabbed my phone, found the connecting cable from my shoulder bag, and plugged my phone into the laptop. The pictures almost immediately started downloading into my photo program—I hadn't realized I'd taken so many. There were well over two hundred of them. I waited until the download was complete, then started working my way through them.

"What people don't realize," I heard my old college roommate, Ashleigh, saying, "is that photographers literally take thousands of pictures rather than simply looking through the lens and waiting for the conditions to be right. They discard all the bad ones. That's why digital photography has changed the business, Ariel. Before, the cost of film was prohibitive, and photographers also had to know how to develop their film themselves to save even more. Now if you want a good picture, you just take as many as you can and then sort through them later. You'll be surprised at what the camera can catch that you didn't see."

There was, of course, more to being a good photographer than that, but it was an excellent crash course for me. I used to spend a lot of time trying to frame the shot and getting everything right before snapping the picture, but now I just pointed the lens and just snapped away rapid-fire. And Ashleigh had been right—I was often surprised at what I found when I downloaded the pictures. I'd had some of my pictures mounted and framed, and I'd begun to love taking pictures as a hobby. It was also incredibly helpful for my work—I could take a lot of pictures of rooms and houses I was working on, at different times of the day, to understand how light worked in the rooms and what designs would best work with the light to create a comfortable atmosphere for my clients.

And someday, when I had more time, I planned on taking some classes, to learn about lighting and angles. I enjoyed taking pictures—why not learn how to be the best photographer I could?

Something else you could have done when you were a Real Housewife of Sea Oats, I thought as I clicked on the first picture and began scrolling through, choosing which ones to keep and which to discard. I found the ones I was thinking about sending to my client about halfway through the roll, and moved them into a folder that I gave her name. I kept working my way through the other pictures, discarding most of them—there wasn't anything else I could have used them for—and then, when I was getting near the end of the sequence I stopped and stared at the computer screen.

Was that—*Angus*?

I clicked to enlarge the image.

I remembered turning slowly and holding down the home button, snapping rapid-fire photos while I turned 360 degrees, not paying attention to anything other than the light and shadows, how the shades of green changed depending on the lighting and how they contrasted yet blended together—that was what I was trying to capture in the images, and I'd focused on that, not noticing anything else, not paying attention in my single-mindedness.

But yes, that was definitely Angus I'd caught in the picture. He was standing just at the corner of the hedge maze, turned away from me, facing someone—or something—just out of the range of my lens. His facial expression—I focused on that part of the image and blew it up even larger. Of course, the larger the image became the blurrier and more pixilated his face became, but the look on his face was unmistakable. He was angry.

I leaned back against the pillows and thought back.

He hadn't seemed angry when he talked to me, had he?

I tried to remember our exchange. He'd startled me, and he had seemed strange to me—happy to see me, but also trying to tell me something.

The truth is in the center of the maze, Miss Ariel, in the center of the maze.

I hadn't heard arguing voices, either. I hadn't heard anything at all before he'd startled me—and I'd heard Charlotte and Peggy quite clearly before I'd seen them. So if he'd been angry and arguing with someone, they'd been whispering, or talking so quietly I couldn't hear them.

Which was also odd.

And he hadn't seem angry at all during our brief interaction, at least not so I'd notice. I'd been thinking about Charlotte and the confrontation we'd just had, stinging from her absolute lack of concern about my presence. Just thinking about it again made my face flush. Leave it to Charlotte—out of all the possible dramatic scenarios I'd pictured when thinking about seeing her again, she'd reacted in the one way I'd not anticipated.

Complete indifference.

No matter what anyone says, the opposite of love isn't hate…it's indifference.

Yes, our marriage was over, except for the legal formalities.

My eyes were dry.

I'd reached acceptance.

That was progress, wasn't it?

I picked up my laptop again, staring at the picture.

Angus had been murdered shortly after I'd taken it. And yes, the more I looked, the more I was certain, he was angry, all right. I could tell by the way his arms were positioned—he always gesticulated with his arms when he was angry.

I moved on to the next picture and yes, same facial expression, his arms in a slightly different place. He was arguing with someone.

I hadn't heard anything, so whoever he was arguing with, they'd kept their voices down. Why? They couldn't have known I was there, or that anyone could overhear them.

Why was it so important to both of them to not be heard?

I kept moving through the pictures, and then—the very last one.

There was a shadow there, someone standing very near to Angus, but the image wasn't clear. I tried blowing it up to a larger size, but was frustrated. Blowing up the picture only made the image blurrier. I copied the image so I could try some of my limited photo editing skills on it later, but I was certain identifying the person was beyond my capabilities.

But surely the police would be able to do something with it? Didn't they have computer techs working for them?

I looked for the cop's card but couldn't find it at first, finally finding it crumpled up inside the front pocket of the jeans I'd worn yesterday.

There was an email address.

I was about to start attaching the images when my door opened and Kayla slipped through, shutting it behind her.

She looked like she'd just woken up, and that was even more annoying than her coming into my room without knocking. She wasn't wearing any makeup, and her skin still glowed, even in the crappy lighting in my room. She pulled the red-blond hair back from her face into a ponytail and was wearing a *Hamilton* sweatshirt with the neck cut so it fell over her bare shoulder, and the rest cut off just below her breasts to show off a flat stomach, a navel pierced with a diamond stud, and a waist so tiny I hoped it meant she lived on nuts and berries only. Her jean shorts were cut incredibly short to show off her long, tanned legs. She had a catlike face, coming to a pointed tip at her chin, and her greenish-hazel eyes were also catlike. She had a snub nose, pale pink lips, and a wide mouth, everything on her face hanging from prominent cheekbones. She was beautiful, I supposed, in an aesthetically pleasing way, and I could see how those features would pop in photographs. But she didn't do anything for me.

She yawned as she ungracefully plopped down on the end of the bed where Peggy had so recently been sitting. "Morning." She stretched and smiled lazily at me. "You don't have anything to eat in here, do you?"

I laughed. "No, why would I? Just go down to the kitchen. Maeve'll make you something to eat."

She made a face. "That housekeeper woman doesn't approve of me. She thinks I'm lazy."

I smothered a grin. Maeve had definite ideas about working hard, and more than once I'd heard her lecture Bast about sleeping late. "She won't let you starve even if she thinks you sleep too late," I said. "Don't you have early morning calls as a model?"

"I can never fall asleep before three." She yawned again. "I just nap if I have an early morning shoot, and then nap during the day whenever I can." She giggled. "But if I have a choice I'll sleep all day."

"You and Bast are definitely suited for one another," I observed.

"We are," she replied, giving me an impudent grin. "That's why I'm going to last and the others didn't. Bast and I understand each other. That's why most couples fail—they don't understand each other."

"Really," I replied, but she had a point. Charlotte and I had never understood each other, had we, and look at where we'd found ourselves.

"Once Bast gets his money troubles under control, we're getting married." She hugged her knees, and looked about thirteen years old. She gave me a sly look. "I love him, but"— she hesitated—"but I'm not going to take on all that debt. I'm keeping my money separate from his." She tilted her head defiantly. "He's not very good with money."

"That's smart of you. And you're right, he's never been good with money." I wondered how much she knew about what was going on at Sea Oats. "Do you know the details of his money trouble?"

She sighed and collapsed back on the bed, the cut-off sweatshirt rising up over her rib cage and exposing the bottom of her firm breasts. "He borrowed money to invest in some company, supposed to be some sure thing—a dating app, or something like that—I didn't pay a lot of attention to it other than I gave it to my financial adviser and he said for me not to give them a cent, it was too risky, and I told Bast that but he wouldn't listen to me." She gave me a look. "Because I'm a model, and you know, models are *stupid* so no one ever listens to us." She rolled her eyes. "I may not have a degree or gone to college, but I'm not stupid about money." She licked her lower lip. "I grew up poor and I'm not ever going back to that."

"I don't blame you."

"Modeling is hard work." She sat back up again, the sweatshirt settling downward. "Sure, you have to be pretty, and be photogenic, but that doesn't mean it's easy."

"I never said it was."

"And I work too hard, and I've worked too long, to let my husband get his hands on my money."

"Do you plan on keeping working after you marry Bast?" It was hard for me to imagine Bast getting married, but he could do much worse than Kayla. Marrying her might be the best thing for him, in fact.

"He's so bad with money I'll have to, won't I?" She laughed, like the sound of tinkling glass. "But that's fine. I don't mind supporting us both."

"Supporting?" I stared at her. "It's that bad, then?"

"He borrowed a ridiculous amount of money and had to use his shares of the company as collateral for the loan." She shook her head, the ponytail bouncing. "Poor Bast, it's always bothered him that Charlotte is so smart and successful. He's always trying to prove he's just as good at business as she is, and that's going to be what ruins him in the end, you know? If he would just accept that he is good at different things and would stop trying to prove himself, he wouldn't get into these messes she has to bail him out of, you know, and then he wouldn't have to try to prove himself again, and it's this whole big cycle of failure and it's going to keep going until he breaks the cycle." She crossed her arms. "I'm going to get him to stop, you know."

"I thought the company trusts were set up so he couldn't do this?" Charlotte had told me once that her grandfather had set up everything so that the capital was always preserved, no matter how bad the mistakes the members of the family made. He'd done this because his two brothers had blown through their shares of the family money in a matter of years, winding up broke and living off his largesse. Maybe something had changed, or Charlotte hadn't explained it completely to me. I'd never understood all the ins and outs of how the trusts and the company worked. It was complicated, and I was glad my own work responsibilities didn't include managing the business side of the firm. Hollis once told me her brain was a spreadsheet and her heart a calculator, and she was right. Hollis might not have been the most creative or talented designer in the world, but she was one of the smartest, building up a brand that made her firm one of the most sought-after interior design firms in the country. She was also planning on expanding that brand into furniture design as well, but that was still on the drawing board.

"I don't know. I don't think Bast knows for sure, but all I know is he owes a lot of money, and if he doesn't pay the money back the bank is going to take his shares of the company."

And if someone was trying to take control of Swann's by buying up shares...Bast's block was significant enough that Charlotte wouldn't be able to keep control.

No wonder she was so stressed.

I bet Roger could explain it all to me better. He'd been an investment banker, after all, and when some of the Swann's stock was taken public he'd handled it all, making himself a small fortune in the process.

"What are you looking at?" Kayla was staring at my computer screen.

I closed it. "I took a lot of pictures of the grounds yesterday when I was out walking," I replied casually. "I was just going through them."

"That looked like Angus." She wrapped her arms around herself. "That's kind of creepy, don't you think? Right before he was killed and all? What was that blurry shadow?"

"Nothing, probably."

Her eyes opened wide. "Maybe you took a picture of the killer!"

"No," I replied, keeping my voice calm. "And even if I did, it's too blurry to make out."

She got up. "Well, I'm going to go brave the kitchen." She paused at the door. "Keep an eye out for Bast, won't you?"

Chapter Seven

I'd grown up in a world as far divorced from Sea Oats and New York City as possible. I was the only child of two parents who'd never left Kansas before I was born, and considered big cities dangerous and scary places. The suburban town in Kansas where I'd spent almost my entire childhood waiting to escape was the kind of place most politicians, trying to drum up populist support, called the real America—even though they spent as little time there as they could, rousing the rabble until their votes were secured, disappearing again until the votes were needed again. Neither of my parents had gone to college, and didn't think I needed to go; what I needed was to find the right man to marry and father my children. My going away to school in New York and deciding to settle there was as alien to them as my coming out to them and when I'd married Charlotte.

I hadn't spoken to either of them in years. There wasn't any point. They believed I was going through a phase I'd wake up from one day, find a nice man, and be a good little housewife with a house full of grandchildren for them. There was nothing I could say that would convince them otherwise.

They'd die waiting, apparently.

My mother might not have a college education, and might

have been mired in her religious belief that people like me were going straight to hell when we died, but she could be wise about some things. She'd always told me that facing my fears, for example, was better than just worrying about them. *The reality is never as bad as you can imagine it*, she always said to me, whether it was apologizing to a friend I'd wronged or breaking up with whatever boy I was going steady with, or talking to a teacher about a failed assignment.

So when I heard the roar of a car in the driveway and looked out to see the little red convertible MG parked out in front and Sebastian climbing out, I knew I had to go down and face him.

Facing him couldn't be any worse than facing his sister had been.

Sebastian Swann, like his sister, had always been a handsome man; when he was a child he was so breathtakingly pretty he could have modeled. From the pictures I'd seen, he'd never had an awkward phase, either, when his face was covered in pimples or his arms and legs had grown crazily out of proportion to the rest of him, or had to wear braces to straighten his teeth. No, Sebastian had been blessed by Mother Nature from birth, and he also had an older sister and an older cousin to baby and spoil him, make much of him, make him feel like he was special and the rules didn't apply to him.

And people had always treated him better because of his looks.

Everything had come easily to him because he was so exceptionally good looking, and having money didn't hurt, either. It was one of the sad secrets of our modern society that life was often easier for those of us with the good fortune to be better looking than others. Beauty brought privilege with it, just as money did.

The privilege could be subtle, and unnoticeable: little

things like getting served first at the bar, or getting helped almost immediately in a department store, with sales clerks hovering over you, or the unawareness of how easy it was to get a cab to stop for you on a busy street during rush hour. It could also be blatant: having teachers fawn on you and favor you, how popularity always seemed to go with the beauty, how people were always ready to do you favors and carry your books and walk you home or buy you a drink.

The good-looking people were, of course, unaware of these extra benefits of their beauty, of the subtle privileges that came with it, and often took these things for granted. Very few of them were conscious of how blessed they were, only about how they were envied.

As the only boy and the youngest Swann, Sebastian had been spoiled almost from birth; fussed over by not only his parents but his adoring older sister and cousin. But unfortunately, the coddling had a negative effect on his personality. He was used to getting what he wanted, and when he was thwarted, he could be petty and spiteful and mean. He was arrogant, and could be caustic when the mood struck him. He expected people to cave in to him, to give him what he wanted without question, and woe to the fool who didn't.

I'd heard stories, of course, about girls from lower-class families he'd seduced, abortions Peggy had paid for, checks written to get those girls to vanish in the night. Sebastian spent money like there was an infinite supply of it, on clothes and gifts and cars. He had a lavish penthouse on the Upper West Side of Manhattan, where hangers-on and lickspittles pretending to be his friends gathered for debauched parties where champagne flowed and drugs were in abundant supply. His exploits were detailed in gossip columns and tabloids; he'd gotten into fights with celebrities, had a celebrated feud with a young rising star who had once been a drinking buddy. He closed nightclubs, walked red carpets with a series of disposable beautiful women on his arm, and had broken thousands of hearts. He'd almost married a recording superstar, but the engagement ended when she caught him in her bed with her personal assistant.

It should go without saying that they were both kicked out of her life, and the recording artist moved on quickly to another boy toy, and replaced the female PA with a gay man—no one could say she didn't learn from her mistakes.

The accepted story within the family was that he'd been kicked out of boarding schools and flunked out of numerous colleges because he was so clever and smart, he bored easily, and he acted out when he was bored. Peggy had explained this to me so many times I could recite the litany along with her. I'd even heard a version of it from Charlotte—but in fairness, it sounded rote when she said it, as though it was something she'd said so many times she didn't even have to think about it. I wasn't even certain she believed it herself anymore. God knows, Char had cleaned up enormous messes created by Sebastian's carelessness and selfishness over the years. He was her brother and she loved him, but they were still siblings, and there was an element of competitiveness and rivalry between them.

For me, it seemed like Sebastian was always trying to prove himself as smart and savvy as his sister. It always backfired on him, because he wasn't. He wasn't stupid by any means—he actually was quite clever and witty and smart—but he never used his intelligence to get ahead in the world.

Rather, he used it for malice.

And how well I knew that!

He had his back to me as I stood in the doorway to the second drawing room, the one with the wet bar that the family used, with the connecting pocket doors to the dining room.

This room had originally been the one, back when Arabella

was mistress of the house, where the ladies had withdrawn after a sumptuous dinner, to sip their tasteful little crystal glasses of sherry and where they could gossip while the men had their brandy and cigars and talked about manly things in the other room, across the hall. If the other drawing room had been Samuel's domain, and the décor matched his taste, then this one was all Arabella's. She'd decorated it accordingly, and it was one of my favorite rooms in the house. Even so many years later, there was still a touch of the feminine in the room so sorely absent from the other drawing room. The color palette here was softer pastels, the furniture more about comfort and relaxation—nowhere in this room was the aggressive, masculine style that made the matching drawing room so unpleasant.

The Sargent painting of Arabella in her later years over the fireplace, after years of widowhood, was one of my favorite paintings in the house. Her black widow's weeds, the lines and the sagging chin of the older woman, were belied by the mischievous smile and youthful sparkle in her eyes. Her dress was a widow's black, of course, but ropes of pearls hung around her neck and enormous diamonds flashed on her plump fingers. Her gray hair was long and worn down in the painting, given her a sense of informality unusual in Sargent's paintings. She seemed almost alive and vibrant, like she was just about to join in the conversation with some bon mot that would have everyone laughing at her wit.

The painting had always made me feel welcome in the room, even when Sea Oats hadn't felt like my home. It was no wonder it was one of my favorites.

The clink of ice in a rocks glass was unmistakable. It wasn't even quite two in the afternoon and he was already making himself a drink.

I stood, watching him silently, not saying anything,

thinking, remembering. He looked much the same from behind as he had two years earlier. He was wearing a navy blue collared polo shirt that showed off his broad shoulders. His waist wasn't quite as narrow as it had been two years earlier, and his jeans looked a bit too tight, like he needed to go up a size but his male vanity refused to admit it. His reddish blond hair looked a little brassy in the light, like it wasn't natural anymore—he'd always worn it longer than I thought he should, and I couldn't help but wonder if he was coloring it. Charlotte had started to gray much younger than he was now...

He'd modeled for a while when he was in his early twenties, but had gotten bored with it quickly and given it up—like everything else he'd tried.

What was it the gossip columns called him? Oh, yes, a *playboy entrepreneur.*

Because they couldn't say spoiled rich wastrel, which was more honest.

He'd been very kind to me when Charlotte brought me home as her wife.

Sea Oats had overwhelmed me. About three weeks before we were married, Charlotte had taken me out there for a weekend—which was when we'd seen the swans on the pond. That first visit to Sea Oats had been the capper to what I was already thinking of in terms of fairy tales: Charlotte was my Disney prince, Sea Oats was her castle, and I was the princess, born to a humble family but oh so deserving.

Working for Hollis had made me a bit blasé about Manhattan wealth; I'd worked on any number of stunning apartments, condos, and brownstones all over the island, even though I was still relatively new to the interior design business. That first time I'd laid eyes on Sea Oats, I couldn't stop myself from staring. I'd done as much research as I could on the Swann family and their company before I'd gone to work on Charlotte's offices in the Swann building, and God knew I'd shopped at Swann's enough times; Swann's had been my first credit card. I knew there was money—the budget on the redesign of the offices alone was astronomical, and my commission was more than I'd made the previous year—but even when you know, you don't until you can see it.

Sea Oats was enormous, and no amount of Google searching online could have prepared me for the reality of the huge old Victorian house, with its scrollwork balconies and the round tower in the front with the peaked witch's cap on top of it; the widow's walk with the wrought-iron lace railing, the enormous windows, the rolling lawns, the fountains, and the hedge maze lurking behind the house. Riding in the big town car through the gates with Philip at the wheel and Char sitting next to me, holding my hand and beaming with pride at the look on my face when I saw her home for the first time, had been like something out of every rags-to-riches romantic comedy movie I'd ever watched repeatedly back in Kansas, dreaming of the day when that would become my reality.

"Look, are those swans on the pond? You keep swans?" I said, looking out the car window as it went around the curve in the driveway, and Charlotte's grip tightened on my hand.

"No, we don't," she whispered, brushing my cheek with her lips. "There's a legend about the pond and swans, you know. When Arabella first saw this property where Samuel meant to build her a house, there were swans on the pond. They both saw it as a sign, and Arabella insisted the pond be kept." She smiled. "Over the years, you know, we've kind of made a legend about the pond and swans. I've always thought it was silly, in a way."

"Why?" I asked as the car stopped.

"Take our bags in, Philip, please," she said as we climbed

out of the car, giving me that brilliant smile that always made me warm inside. "Why don't we walk down to the pond and watch the swans?"

I smiled back at her, gripped her hand tightly as she led me down the flagstone path leading to the pond. "So, what's the legend about the pond?"

"And the swans," she replied, pulling me closer and putting her arm around my waist. "There are rarely swans there, for some reason. We've never tried to keep swans, of course, because Arabella wanted wild swans to use the pond... like the wild swans there the first time she came here. So we've always considered it good luck whenever swans appear there. Good luck, or good fortune, or someone in the family is going to find love."

"Love?" I said, half teasingly.

"My entire life," she said, sinking to one knee in front of me as I watched the swans paddling about the surface of the murky water, "I've never seen a swan on the pond. And the day I bring you here for the first time, there they are. It's like it was meant to be." And she produced the box with my engagement ring, and asked me to marry her there, on the shoreline of the pond as the swan family glided over the top of the water.

And I'd said yes, of course, even though I'd known her for such a short time, even though I had no idea of what being her wife would entail.

It was my Disney cartoon come to life, after all, and who was I to argue with fate?

The swans were a sign. They had to be, right?

I was so young and naïve.

I was terrified that entire weekend I would break something, or do something incredibly gauche that would embarrass Charlotte, cause her to take back the ring and break up with me once we got back to the city. Peggy couldn't have been lovelier on that visit, but Bast was on the West Coast, involved in a relationship with a volatile and deeply troubled former child star that was splashed all over the tabloids and the entertainment news. We didn't talk about Bast much that weekend, or before we were married; Charlotte would just sigh when his name came up and would say, "You'll understand when you meet him," and change the subject.

After that weekend and its surprise proposal, we decided we didn't need a big wedding—I'd dreamed about my wedding as a little girl, but as an adult it didn't seem that important to me. Instead, we rushed down to City Hall a few weeks later to marry in haste, and after tying up all the odds and ends the sudden marriage created—letting my roommates know I was giving up the apartment, giving Hollis proper notice, boxing up my stuff in both my office and home—we'd gone off to Italy for a two-week honeymoon in Venice and Florence and Rome, where I was blown away by the beauty of the art and the cities, and I fell in love with all three cities, as millions before me had done.

But if the romance and honeymoon had been a Disney movie, the marriage was anything but. There's a reason you don't ever see Beauty and her Beast after the end of the movie; the day-to-day life of a married couple is anticlimactic after all the obstacles they overcame to find love with each other.

Charlotte and I hadn't had any obstacles to overcome before we were married.

After the honeymoon, though—well, that was a different story.

Bast had been at Sea Oats when we returned from Italy. I was still floating on a cloud of radiance, in love with Charlotte and Italy and life itself. I was going to be the best wife Charlotte could have ever dreamed about having, I decided. She didn't go with me to Sea Oats from the airport—there'd been some emergency with Swann's, so Charlotte had gone directly to the office from JFK. "Sorry," she'd said to me as she kissed me on the cheek as I got into the backseat of the town car, "I'll take a cab to the office. Philip, come back into the city after you get her to Sea Oats, all right? I'm so sorry."

"You don't ever need to apologize to me, we're married," I said to her, melting a little inside at the pleased smile on her face, and then the door was shut and we were pulling away from the curb. I was content, and happy.

Had I only known.

I don't know how Bast could have known we were on our way—maybe Charlotte had called him—but he was waiting for me on the front gallery when the car pulled up. I wasn't expecting to see him there, though I should have suspected he might be there.

There had been a final showdown with the crashing star, who'd wound up going into rehab after an arrest for public intoxication and possession of cocaine. It was all over the tabloids—even in Italy, we hadn't been able to escape Bast's latest scandal. Charlotte refused to talk about it, just saying, "You'll learn about Bast soon enough."

Bast had, as always, returned to Sea Oats after getting off the roller coaster. He very graciously—or so I'd thought at the time—befriended me, made me feel at home. Peggy did as well, but she was often busy seeing to the house and to the numerous charity boards she worked on. So it fell to Bast to fill my time, keep me company, take me on walks around the estate, tell me family history, gossip, and lore, to be my friend—and of course, fill me in on Charlotte's troubled past with Lindsay Moore.

I'd thought Bast was my friend.

It wasn't the first time I'd trusted the wrong person.

"Hello, Bast," I said calmly. "How nice to see you, after all this time."

He finished pouring his whiskey and turned around, a big smile on his florid face. "Darling Ariel, I'd heard you'd come back. I didn't think I would ever see you again, you know, after you ran away screaming into the night." He took a drink, his eyes still on me, glittering malevolently.

The two years I'd been gone hadn't been kind to Bast. Another one of my mother's favorite sayings was, *The young are all beautiful, but when you get older you get the face you deserve.* I'd always thought it kind of a harsh thing to say, but the effortless beauty Bast had been blessed with since birth was beginning to fade. His body had started to go to seed, and it was clear he didn't care much. His body, once toned and muscled from hours of work in the gym with trainers, looked soft from the front, and there was a bit of a paunch to his stomach. His reddish-gold hair, always so thick and full, like Charlotte's, was thinner in the front and the bangs were grown longer and brushed across his forehead in a vain attempt to make it look smaller. There were bags, angry and purplish, under the reddened eyes, and a second chin was starting to sprout just below his once strong jawline. The years of long nights spent partying and doing whatever drug was readily available were now showing on his face. It wasn't too late—if he stopped drinking and staying up all night, and instead started going to the gym more regularly, he could get it all back.

But I suspected Bast didn't want to work hard. He never had before, so why would he start now?

It was a pity, because Sebastian had been so handsome, still had been when I'd last seen him. I always looked away when I saw him in tabloids or magazines, turning the page quickly or putting the publication away because seeing him reopened the wounds I was trying to heal. Had his decline been sudden? Had this already started when I'd been at Sea Oats before, and had I just not noticed because I was so dazzled by everything, so insecure and afraid of everything?

"You look good." He toasted me with the glass, now half empty. "When I saw you in the style section a couple of weeks ago, I thought, damn, getting away from the Swanns has done her a world of good. Smartest decision you ever made, wasn't it?" He finished the whiskey and poured another.

"You could say that." I sat down on one of the couches, never taking my eyes off him. "Your current girl is lovely. I like her."

He sat down on the couch facing mine, put the glass down on the coffee table without a coaster. Peggy would have had a fit. When I'd lived here, I would have said something, but it wasn't my house anymore and it wasn't my problem. His face lit up with a smile, and for a moment he seemed younger, his old self, again. "Kayla's great, isn't she?"

I crossed my legs. "She tells me you're getting married. Once your current misfortune is handled, of course."

He glowered at me. "My situation isn't any of your business."

"I suppose not." I looked at him, trying to find any trace of remorse. I couldn't see any, of course, which didn't surprise me. Bast had always been amoral. What Bast had done to me and Charlotte—he probably hadn't given it a second thought once I'd left Sea Oats. He'd wrecked our lives, our marriage, and done it deliberately. I'd been an idiot to trust him, to think he was my friend, when the entire time he was also feeding lies to Charlotte about me, hints and insinuations, so that final night, when she'd caught him kissing me on the mouth— well, she'd seen something else entirely than what it was, an unwanted kiss from a man. There was nothing I could say that could change her mind, make her understand that Bast was just a friend to me, would never be anything more than that, couldn't be. I wasn't wired that way, to be attracted to men.

I thought she'd known that.

But her experiences with Lindsay Moore—those hurts, wounds, had run far deeper than I could have imagined. I thought Charlotte was strong and believed in my love for her.

It hurt that she didn't believe me. It hurt that she thought I could do such a thing.

And the hurt had turned into anger.

But we'd done nothing but fight those last few weeks. A lot of it was my fault, my insecurities—which Bast had also been playing on. I knew now Lindsay had meant nothing to Charlotte back then, but I'd been jealous. Bast knew how to twist the knife without me even being aware I'd been stabbed yet.

And now he sat there, smiling at me, like we were old friends and he'd never done anything.

What must it be like to not have a conscience, I wondered. Bast had probably convinced himself in the meantime he'd done nothing, that I'd thrown myself at him the way other women always had.

I'd been such a fool to think him a friend.

I wouldn't make that mistake again.

I wanted to slap him right across that smug face.

"What brings you back to Sea Oats after all this time?" he asked casually. "I thought you were done with us once and for all."

I gave him a sour smile. "Peggy emailed me, told me I was needed." I gestured with my right hand. "And now I can't leave, because of the police investigation. I'd be gone already if I had any say in it."

"Angus." He made a face, and I remembered Angus hadn't been a fan of Bast, unlike everyone else at Sea Oats. There had been something—Bast had done something to the maze when he was a teenager, played some prank, which had infuriated Angus, and Angus never forgot or forgave him for it. Angus was the one person Bast couldn't charm. "Who'd want to kill that old fool? He should have retired years ago, anyway."

"And the fire, don't forget the fire." I watched him as I spoke, to see how he reacted.

I wouldn't put it past him to have had something to do with all of it.

He shook his head, but I could see the hand holding his glass was shaking slightly. A sign of guilt? Did Bast know more than he was letting on?

It was convenient, after all, that he didn't show up at Sea Oats until after everything happened.

I wouldn't have thought Bast capable of murder two years ago, but now I wasn't sure if there was anything he wasn't capable of.

"Who are these people you owe money to, Sebastian?" He'd always hated it when I called him by his full name. "Are they dangerous?"

He paled. "You don't know what you're talking about."

I stood up. "I don't put anything past you, Bast."

"That's no way to talk to a friend—"

"We aren't friends, Bast. That ship sailed." It was a great exit line, so I took advantage of it to walk out of the drawing room. I was halfway up the stairs to the second floor when I had to stop because I'd started shaking. I grabbed onto the railing and closed my eyes, willing myself to get a grip.

It was closure of a sort, I supposed. Maybe not the way I would have wanted it—I would have much preferred him on his knees, tears streaming down his face, confessing to everything he'd done and begging my forgiveness, but I'd known that wasn't ever going to happen other than in my fantasies. But I knew now I could be in the same room with him without slapping him or wanting to kill him, which was progress.

When I reached the second floor I decided to stop into the library to get something to read. The fireplace was going, and it was starting to rain again outside. Dustin Rockwell was seated at one of the tables, reading an enormous old volume with papers spread all around the table. He looked up when I opened the door and smiled. "Ariel! Come in, have a seat."

"I don't want to disturb you," I replied, but walked over to his table anyway. "What are you reading?"

He held up the book so I could read the spine. *The History of Penobscot* by Scott Chandler.

"I've never heard of that book," I said, slipping into a chair on the other side of the table from him.

He laughed. "It's not like it was a runaway best seller. The Historical Society published it last year. It's little more than a glorified fairy tale about the town and the Swanns." He placed a bookmark in it and closed it. "It's what it doesn't say that interests me, of course." He winked. "Arabella Swann was hardly a saint, no matter what people around here want to think. Maybe I shouldn't mention this to you, as a member of the family—"

"Not for long." I corrected him. "Charlotte and I are going to be divorced eventually."

"Ah, yes, the divorce." He smile got even wider. "We'll get around to that. Did you know that one of Arabella's sons knocked up one of the maids?"

He'd succeeded in surprising me. "No, I didn't know that."

"I can't imagine it was one of those stories that the family sat around at dinner discussing." He laughed. "But yes, it did happen. I've been trying to find what happened to the maid and her child. But Arabella paid them off and sent them away—no son of hers was going to marry a maid. So there's a collateral branch of Swanns out there somewhere."

"I would imagine there's more than one," I said. "There have been lots of Swann males over the years, and where there are spoiled heirs, there are usually mistresses and children somewhere."

"So cynical for one so young." He winked at me. "I gather Sebastian has arrived?"

I nodded. "Yes. What did you mean about my divorce?"

"Did you, by any chance, sign a prenuptial agreement when you married Charlotte? Or is that too personal a question?"

"No, it's not too personal, and no, I didn't. We got married quickly." I closed my eyes. "I did have to sign some papers regarding the Swann trusts after we got married, but no, I never signed a prenup."

"That makes things even more interesting, then." He narrowed his eyes. "You know Sebastian Swann owes a lot of money, and that he put up his shares in Swann's to guarantee the loans, right?"

"Yes, and I don't understand," I replied. "I was always under the impression that the trust was created in order to keep control of the company within the family, even after Charlotte took the company public. It's too complicated for me to understand, but I don't get how he was able to do that."

"What you don't understand," he replied softly, "is that the trust controlling the corporate stock officially was dissolved when Charlotte wanted to take the company public, several years before you married her. The family trusts still exist— that was why Sebastian had to put up his stock. Charlotte is trustee and wouldn't let him have the money."

"So why doesn't she just pay off the loans with money from the trust?"

"Because it's too much money." He shook his head again. "And you know, as Charlotte's wife, you have a claim to her shares of the company."

"I don't want anything to do with that."

But as I said the words, it clicked in my head.

Someone was trying to take over Swann's. If Sebastian's stock wasn't forfeited...as Charlotte's wife I might make a legal claim on her shares.

And I might cooperate with whoever was behind the hostile takeover.

That was why Peggy had sent for me.

CHAPTER EIGHT

A t any time over the past two years, had someone told me that I would have dinner with Lindsay Moore, I would have laughed them out of the room. If they would have added that the dinner was at her home and she'd invited me, I would have laughed even harder. There was no love lost between the two of us. When I'd first met her, I knew all about her—Bast had happily filled me in on the woman who'd been involved, off and on, with my wife for most of their lives. But I'd been determined to be gracious, to be friends, to offer an olive branch and make what was bound to be an uncomfortable situation as easy on her as possible.

God, I'd been young and naïve.

The first thing she'd said to me, after Peggy introduced us at a fundraiser for the Penobscot Library, was, after giving me a good looking over, "Well, this isn't going to last." She'd smirked at me. "Enjoy Sea Oats while you can. You'll be gone soon enough."

Even remembering it now made my cheeks grow hot. I'd avoided her and her acid tongue as much as I could that year at Sea Oats, but what was the most galling about remembering it was that she'd been right.

She knew Charlotte better than I ever would.

Well, I thought as I looked out the window as the town car pulled into the driveway of her house, *you're welcome to Charlotte, Lindsay, and I hope you two make each other miserable.*

My tension must have been obvious, because Kayla took my hand and squeezed it gently. "Don't be nervous, Ariel, she's nobody to Charlotte," she whispered with a sidelong glance at Bast, sitting on her other side in the backseat of the big town car. "And no one can hurt you unless you let them have that power over you."

Bast snorted. "Lindsay's no ordinary woman, Kayla, and the sooner you realize that, the better off you'll be."

Kayla stuck her tongue out at him and smiled back at me. I smothered a laugh. I liked her, and hoped she didn't wind up as just another notch on his worn-out belt.

I squeezed her hand back. "Thanks, Kayla, I appreciate the moral support, but I'll be fine. And no matter what Bast says, Lindsay is very ordinary."

He scowled back at me.

Lindsay had called Sea Oats during lunch. Maeve had served us homemade potato-leek soup and a fresh garden salad. Peggy didn't join us—she was having lunch at the Historical Society in town—and so it was just Kayla, Bast, and me in the dining room. It could have been awkward, but nothing could be awkward with Kayla around. She filled the pregnant pauses and heavy silences with endless prattle about modeling gigs she'd had and gossip about famous people—some I'd heard of, others I hadn't—and some of the stories were quite funny. Kayla was a gifted storyteller, and she could do voices and mimic accents like a professional. It was hard to be tense when someone was being so funny.

Maeve came in to tell me there was a call for me, which was a surprise. I got up from the table, confused, and she handed me the cordless phone in the hallway. Not many people knew I was at Sea Oats, and those that did—Hollis, a client, or someone else from the office—would have called my cell phone. "Hello?" I said. "This is Ariel."

"Ariel, it's Lindsay Moore." I would have recognized the low, throaty voice even if she hadn't said her name. Her voice was distinctive, and sexy. She could have made a killing doing the voice of cartoon femme fatales. "I'd heard you were back at Sea Oats"—*I just bet you heard*—"and would love to catch up with you. Would you be open to coming over for dinner tonight? Around eight?"

"Um, sure." I was so surprised I just blurted it out.

"I understand Bast and his latest are there, as well. Can you invite them?"

"Just a moment, and I'll ask," I replied, walking back into the dining room. As I asked them if they were interested, I realized what she was after with this invitation. If she was trying to get back together with Charlotte, she wanted to see how much of a threat I was. It probably shook her up a little to hear I was back at Sea Oats. I should have gotten back on the phone and told her no, but if this trip was about closure, I was going to get it from anyone I could.

If that meant giving Lindsay the green light to go after Charlotte again was part of getting there, so be it. *More power to you, Lindsay, and I wish you both all the happiness the two of you deserve, may you both live happily ever after.*

But it was much easier to think than believe.

Understandably, I'd never been to Lindsay's home before. I only ran into her at fundraisers or parties when I'd been living here before, and we made the effort to stay out of each other's way as much as possible. It wasn't until I was gone that I realized seeing me was probably even harder for her than seeing her was for me, but it didn't make me like her any more. She'd always, on those rare occasions when we had run into each other, been cutting and borderline insulting to me. Whenever I'd complained about her to Charlotte, Charlotte would always take her side—well, maybe not take her side, but that was how it seemed to me at the time. Charlotte expected me to be more sympathetic, understanding, to Lindsay, and I saw that as her being on Lindsay's side.

We'd had more than one argument because of Lindsay.

She lived on the other side of Penobscot from Sea Oats. The house was inland, didn't have a beach or even a view of the ocean. The Moores had long since lost their family businesses, and Lindsay's father had been upper-level management for Swann's, and a close friend of Charlotte and Bast's father. Lindsay had grown up with both Char and Bast, had grown up thinking of Sea Oats as her second home.

It was no wonder she felt she had a right to the house.

Charlotte had never told me about her romantic involvement with Lindsay, simply dismissing it as "nothing serious, something in the past you don't need to worry about."

Bast, on the other hand, had been more than happy to fill me in on the decades-long soap opera starring the two of them. "It broke Charlotte's heart when Lindsay got married," he'd told me in the hushed voice of confidences and secrets, "and I'm not sure she ever got over it." Already feeling like I didn't belong at Sea Oats, worried that Charlotte already regretted marrying me, finding out about her past with Lindsay had been yet another crack in the foundation of our marriage.

When I confronted Charlotte about it, she'd lost her patience with me for the first time. "I never told you about her because it doesn't matter!" she'd shouted at me. "She doesn't matter! She's my past! You're my present! I married you!" I had burst into tears and she'd hugged me, kissing me and apologizing for making me cry, but I still believed Lindsay was a threat. No matter how many times she reassured me, promised me, told me that Lindsay didn't matter to her, that it was me she loved, I was too insecure and too young to believe her.

It never occurred to me until later, of course, that playing up their history was part of Bast's game, driving yet another wedge between Char and me, playing on my all-too-obvious insecurities. And he never relented, either, constantly whispering in my ear about how much Charlotte had loved her, how everyone thought they were destined to be together, it wouldn't be fair of him to not let me know, of course, and I was his friend, he cared about me so much and he didn't want to see me hurt.

No, Bast had never been my friend. Bast had wanted me gone, and had done everything he could to make sure it happened. I didn't understand why, probably never would. It was just part of the weird game he and Charlotte always played.

I'm sure a psychiatrist could have a field day with it. But it wasn't my problem anymore. Once I was free to go back into the city, I would get my divorce and wash my hands of the Swanns and their problems. And as for the stock in Swann's, Charlotte could have it. I didn't want anything from her except my freedom.

Lindsay's house was nice, the kind of place someone upper middle class would have built forty years ago, kind of a Tudor-style two-story manor house, long with lots of rooms and a three-car garage. It reminded me of the houses the rich people back in Kansas built for themselves, out near the country club, the houses my mother longed to live in someday. I'd always thought there was something tacky and phony about them, and that was how Lindsay's house struck me at first glance: pretentious, phony, wanting desperately to be something that it wasn't.

I could see why Lindsay would have wanted to be mistress of Sea Oats, and then chided myself for the bitchiness of the thought.

The driveway ended in a circle, around a stone fountain with dancing cherubs and maidens pouring water out of urns, surrounded by a small, low cut hedge. The driveway itself wasn't paved, but was white gravel and oyster shells crunching under the tires. The white gravel sparkled in the moonlight, when the moon came out from behind the dark clouds crowding the night sky. The house didn't have a porch, just a flagstone path from the driveway through empty flower beds to the front door. A large hedge outlined the edge of the property, and it was tall enough to block out the views of the neighboring houses.

It's a nice house, I said to myself, pushing down the bitchy thoughts before they could even form. *And I'm sure it's warm and cozy inside.*

It embarrassed me to remember the way I'd seethed with jealousy of Lindsay, certain that Charlotte often looked at me and found me lacking in comparison.

What a child I'd been. It was a wonder Charlotte hadn't shown me the door months before I left.

Joseph let us out at the front door. Kayla, shivering in a too short dress that barely covered her ass, bounded up the walk quickly to knock on the door, which opened immediately, as if Lindsay had been waiting right there for us to arrive. They exchanged air kisses, she got a hug from Bast, and then it was the two of us, facing each other like gladiators in the arena.

I mentally gritted my teeth and kissed her warm cheek. "Lovely to see you, Lindsay. Thanks again for having us."

"My pleasure, Ariel. You look beautiful, as always." Her tone was cool, cordial, and civil. Maybe this wouldn't be as awkward and awful as I'd feared. Then again, she was playing from a position of strength. I was out of Charlotte's life, after all.

She led us into her cozy living room.

One thing I couldn't fault Lindsay for was taste. Her living room was large, and of course she had a fire going in the obligatory fireplace. The room was tastefully decorated in muted shades of blue with yellow highlights. The artwork, hung at discreet distances, blended in perfectly with the colors of the walls—so often people make the amateur mistake of choosing art that either clashes with the room or is so powerful that it overpowers the rest of the room. Instead, Lindsay had chosen gorgeous black-and-white images of old New York from the thirties and the forties, mounted simply on white backgrounds with black metal frames. The carpet was thick and soft, dark blue with yellow highlights, and I resisted the urge to ask where she'd gotten it—it would be perfect for a job I was bidding on. The room looked comfortable and cozy, despite its size. An open bottle of red wine with four stemmed glasses sat on a silver serving tray on the coffee table. Kayla and Bast sat on the couch, so I took one of the chairs. It was like sitting on a pillow, and as I sank into it, Kayla passed me a glass of wine. I smiled my thanks.

"Dinner's almost ready," Lindsay said, sitting down in the chair that matched mine. "We should have time for some wine and conversation before the first course."

In the flickering light from the fireplace and the lit candles, Lindsay looked as beautiful as she always had. She had dark hair, cut in waves that fell gently to her shoulders. She wasn't very tall—maybe an inch or two over five feet tall in stocking feet—and she was thin in that way all rich woman aspire to, maybe a size zero, at most a two. She was casually dressed in a red cashmere sweater that hugged her figure—she had nice breasts for so small a woman, and slender hips in her faded skinny jeans and ballet flats. She had a heart-shaped face, coming to a catlike pointed chin, and her skin was tanned, but there was something almost artificial about the tan, like it came from a spray can rather than the sun. Her eyes were large and round and a velvety, expressive brown; her brows were plucked into thin arched lines over them. Her button nose was overwhelmed by her thick lips and a slight underbite. But as she talked and laughed, I noticed that her forehead remained flat and smooth, and the lips didn't look the way they had the last time I saw her. There were other subtle changes to her face—the cheeks a bit fuller than they'd been, and the absence of lines where there should have been made me think she'd had a little bit of work done, here and there. Nothing major, nothing that would be noticeable at first glance, but she was doing her best to fight off the encroaching years with a surgeon's help.

Not that there was anything wrong with that. I liked to think I would just let my face age naturally, wouldn't give in to that kind of vanity, the way Charlotte had. But I didn't yet have lines showing up where there hadn't been any before, and my lips hadn't started getting thinner. Maybe when the lines started cobwebbing out from my mouth and my eyes, when the skin under my chin began to sag ever so lightly, and the lines on my forehead didn't smooth away with a change of expression, my opinions about Botox and fillers and all the little tricks my clients used to look younger might change. The problem I had with these little touches was that they became addictive to women who use them—almost all my clients had work done at some point, and some of them had gone completely overboard—their eyes taking on that telltale slant, the lips too thick, the skin between the nose and upper lip flat and immovable, the mouth line extending past the mouth, the cheeks too plump and too round and too dull, the breasts too large and too perky.

As I'd read somewhere, too much surgery didn't make you look young—it just made you look expensive.

Maybe I would change my mind, but I liked women like Helen Mirren and Judi Dench and Maggie Smith, who wore their age proudly and still looked beautiful and natural and human.

The conversation, both before and during dinner, stayed on easy topics—the weather, Kayla's modeling career, what celebrity was sleeping with whom, the *Real Housewives*, the obligatory talk about the piece on me in the *Times*—and a stranger joining us would have thought it a lovely, civilized dinner, the kind of resounding social success every hostess dreams of and rarely achieves, with warm generous laughter and the kind of easy joking only old friends manage.

But a stranger wouldn't have noticed there was a tension beneath the polite conversation, the gentle laughter, the empty compliments. Every so often, I'd catch Lindsay clutching her wineglass so hard her knuckles turned white, or that her smile didn't quite reach her eyes, or I would catch her staring at me with an intense expression I couldn't quite read on her face. Was it envy, loathing, hatred, curiosity, or something else altogether? I didn't expect Lindsay Moore to like me—I never had, and she never would, even if she managed to marry Charlotte and move into Sea Oats. She just wasn't the kind of woman who could ever be friends with another woman she saw as a rival, and even after the divorce, she would always see me as a rival.

I couldn't blame her for resenting me, if she was in love with Charlotte.

Charlotte wouldn't talk about her past with Lindsay whenever I'd asked her about it—she'd always just waved a hand and said something like, "That was a long time ago," or something similar and dropped the subject. Of course, this just made me even more curious about her, and Peggy wasn't a good source—she hated Lindsay, refused to talk about her, always referred to her as *that woman*. So, naturally I'd turned to Bast, who'd been more than happy to tell me every dirty detail of the long tortured romance.

It was hard to imagine, sitting at her dinner table and making mindless conversation with her, that Lindsay had ever had issues with her own sexuality.

She and Char had first become involved romantically when they were teenagers; Charlotte's parents were already dead by this time so there was, in the Gospel According to Bast, no way of knowing whether they would have been okay with their daughter being a lesbian. It took Peggy some getting used to, but to her, Charlotte was Charlotte and she loved her, so that was the end of that. But Lindsay's parents hadn't been quite so understanding; they'd been more like mine, and I could sympathize with her. Even though I'd made peace with the knowledge I would never have a relationship with my parents again, every now and then—on, say, my birthday, or Mother's Day, or Father's Day, or Thanksgiving, or Christmas—it would hit me again between the eyes like a hammer, and I felt a little sad.

But as time passed, the sadness was for my parents, not for me.

It put them in an awkward place—her father was senior vice president of marketing for Swann's, and even though Charlotte was too young to have any say in the running of the company, she was still part owner, through the trust, and one day she would be running Swann's. So rather than forbidding

Lindsay to see Charlotte, they made things hard on Lindsay, constantly pressuring her to conform, to find a nice guy, to date men, to get married and have children. Like me, she was an only child, so the pressure was amped up even more. Unlike me, she had never escaped from under her parents' thumb...

Which was yet another reason for her to hate me.

Somehow, Lindsay wound up getting married right out of college—shortly after her father retired—and the marriage had been a disaster. Again, according to Bast, she'd been seeing the guy all the while she'd still been involved with Charlotte, who'd had no idea that the love of her life was also seeing a guy. Charlotte had been crushed when Lindsay got married, which was when Peggy turned against Lindsay once and for all. The marriage hadn't lasted long—he drank too much, and apparently when he was drinking he was abusive— and so finally Lindsay had left him and come running home. She'd divorced him, got back with Charlotte, only to marry another man a few years later. That marriage, too, had ended in divorce. Charlotte and Lindsay had then gone on a bout of on-again/off-again that lasted for another few years—

And then Charlotte had married me.

I could certainly relate to Lindsay's issues with her parents. After I came out to them, I only spoke to my family on Thanksgiving, Christmas, and birthdays. When I'd come out to them one summer when I was home from school they'd listened, and when I was finished my mother had just smiled, patted me on the arm, and said, "And we don't ever need to talk about this again, do we?" They remained convinced that I simply hadn't met the right man yet, and once I did, I'd get over this lesbian foolishness once and for all. It was my marriage that ended the détente we'd established. That was when they stopped taking my calls, stopped calling me back, made it clear to me that I wasn't welcome at home.

It was fine. I never wanted to return to Kansas anyway, and the loss of my family—well, I didn't actually lose anything. They didn't love me, they loved their idea of me, and once the façade of that idea was shattered once and for all, they stopped loving me. I'd be lying if I said it hadn't hurt, but it hurt less the more time passed, and now I no longer cared. I wished them well. We kept our respective distances, and we were all better off for it.

I couldn't help but wonder how Lindsay dealt with it.

Lindsay's parents were now living in Florida, and she'd taken over their house. I wasn't sure what she did for money—she couldn't still be supported by her parents—but I knew she also didn't work. Maybe there was a trust or something, I didn't know. It wasn't any of my business.

After the dessert and coffee, Lindsay rose and said to me, "I understand you took some pictures of Angus before he was killed the other day?"

"Um, yes, they're on my phone."

"Angus and I were always close," she said. "Bast, Kayla, do you mind if Ariel and I go off and look at the pictures privately for a few moments?"

I followed her down the hallway to a small room she clearly used as an office. I got out my phone and opened the picture folder, scrolling through the pictures until I found the ones with Angus. She sat down at the desk and I handed her the phone. She turned on the desk light and peered at the pictures, swiping left to get the next ones up. Finally, she handed the phone back to me and said, "You really can't tell who—or what—that is in the picture with him, can you?"

I should have known that was why she wanted to see the pictures. "No, you can't," I replied, slipping my phone back into my purse. "It could be anyone."

"The pictures were just an excuse anyway," she went on. "I wanted to talk to you alone."

"About Charlotte?"

Her face was unreadable. She blinked slowly. "You know Charlotte and I have started seeing each other again?"

"Peggy may have mentioned it." I shrugged. "You don't have anything to worry about, Lindsay. I didn't come back to reconcile with Charlotte, if that's what you're afraid of. That's all over and done with—both Charlotte and I can agree on that, at the very least."

She nodded. "Then why did you come back, Ariel? Couldn't you have just filed for a divorce without coming back here?"

"Peggy sent for me." I was getting tired of all this, and I was beyond tired of covering for Peggy. I'd already told Bast the truth—one of them was bound to tell Charlotte, but that wasn't my problem. I sighed and rolled my eyes. "Apparently, someone is trying a hostile takeover of Swann's, or something like that. I don't really care, honestly. Since I'm married to Charlotte and there was no prenup, Peggy is worried that I have some claim on Charlotte's shares and might side against the family. The whole thing is ridiculous. I have no interest in Swann's and I have even less interest in Charlotte's shares." I held up my hands. "And when I get back to New York, I'm getting a lawyer and getting a divorce. It's long overdue and I don't care what I have to do, but I don't want anything from her. I don't want her money and I don't want her stock and I don't want her company. All I want is my freedom. Is that blunt enough for you?"

"So your being here—it has nothing to do with...with Charlotte?" Her face was vulnerable, and she looked sad and frightened.

"No." I put my hand on her shoulder and squeezed. "Believe me, Lindsay, I get it. I do. If you and Charlotte can make each other happy, more power to the two of you, and I mean that. My marriage was a mistake. I think I can speak for Charlotte in saying that she knows it now just as much as I do. When I go back to the city—when the police will let me go—I'm hiring a lawyer and filing for divorce. I don't know why Charlotte hasn't already. But the marriage is over. I'm not a threat to you."

She laughed bitterly. "Aren't you?"

"No."

"Peggy didn't send for you to try to reconcile?"

"No," I lied. Peggy didn't like Lindsay, had never forgiven her for hurting Charlotte over and over throughout the years. Peggy had brought me out here to break up Lindsay and Charlotte, but no good would come of telling Lindsay that truth. "I didn't even know you two were seeing each other again, honestly."

"It's only been a couple of dinners," Lindsay said. "It may not mean anything. If only—" Her eyes glittered with tears, and for the first time I felt sorry for her, which I am sure was something she would not be happy about.

"Honestly, I wish you both only the best," I lied.

Her eyes narrowed. "Can I see those pictures again?"

I sighed and got my phone back out. I handed it over to her. She squinted at one of the pictures, and held it out to me to see. "Doesn't that—doesn't that kind of look like Peggy?"

"Don't be ridiculous," I replied, glancing at it before putting it back into my purse. Of course, now that she'd said that, I could see how someone might think it was Peggy. There was something about the way the blurred, shadowed figure was standing. But no, it couldn't be Peggy.

Why on earth would Peggy have wanted to kill Angus?

The drive back to Sea Oats was quiet. I looked out my window and no one spoke. Seeing Lindsay had awakened something inside me. I didn't hate her, I didn't resent her anymore. I never should have in the first place. She'd wrecked things with Charlotte several times, and it was little wonder Peggy wanted her out of Charlotte's life once and for all. Peggy was fiercely protective of both Bast and Charlotte. God help poor Kayla if Peggy decided she was wrong for Bast.

I stole a glance over at her. She was resting with her head down on Bast's shoulder, and his arm was around her. Her eyes were closed.

On second thought, Kayla was more than capable of taking care of herself, that was for sure.

I laughed to myself as the car pulled up to the front door of the house. I got out first and didn't wait for the others. I was tired, and just wanted to go straight to bed. I'd had too much wine and my head was swirling, plus I was emotionally exhausted.

What I really wanted to do was pack and get the hell out of there, but that wasn't possible.

But as I was about to go up the staircase to the third floor, Peggy stopped me. "How was dinner?" she asked.

I looked at her. She looked no different than she had before, but I couldn't get Lindsay's suggestion that she was the person in that picture out of my head. How far would Peggy go to protect the family? Would she kill someone she considered a threat?

Of course she would. There was nothing she wouldn't do for either Charlotte or Bast.

But why kill Angus?

I heard him muttering again, the sense of urgency in his voice as he said, *The answer's at the center of the maze. In the center of the maze. Do you know what I mean?*

What was it Bast had done to the maze when he was a teen? That had made Angus angry? I couldn't remember the story…Was Angus trying to tell me that Bast was trouble? To be careful of him?

"It was fine," I replied, keeping my voice steady. "Lindsay was curious why I came back."

"What did you tell her?"

"I didn't tell her you sent for me," I replied. "You did want me to come back here to break them up, didn't you?"

"Charlotte loves you, Ariel. That's all I care about."

I shook my head and continued up the stairs. I opened my door and gasped.

The room was in ruins. My clothes were scattered all over the floor, the bed had been stripped, and the mattress tipped up on its side.

Someone had searched my room.

But why?

My laptop was open on the nightstand.

Grimly, I checked the cloud.

The pictures had been deleted.

CHAPTER NINE

I felt violated.

I got up, sat back down again, closed the laptop, not sure what I should do next. Call for help? Call the police? I stared at the mess in disbelief.

I couldn't call the police.

Whoever did this had access to the house, which meant it was someone staying at Sea Oats. With the security guards Peggy and Char had hired after Angus's murder, no one could have possibly broken into the house. They would have never made it over the fence and across the lawn, for one thing, without being caught.

I started shivering uncontrollably. My underwear was scattered all over the floor. Whoever had done this had handled my underwear.

I wanted to start screaming.

No, no, calm down, Ariel, stop shaking and think, you need to think this through.

I took a few deep breaths. My heart was thumping in my ears, I was sweating.

Angus's killer has access to the house.

Which meant Angus's killer either was a member of the family, or was tied to the Swanns in some way.

I got to my feet, shaking still, grasping onto the bedpost for support. I couldn't stay in the room alone, I didn't want to be alone, I needed someone to be with me.

Kayla.

Her room was just down the hallway.

Somehow I managed to make it to the doorway. The hall stretched out, empty, the lights in their sconces on the walls giving off white light, but there was darkness in places... places where I couldn't tell if someone was lying in wait for me, waiting for me to come out into the hallway.

You're being ridiculous, stop that, you're scaring yourself.

I took another deep breath and stepped out into the hallway. I was still shaking—I didn't think the trembling was ever going to go away, I was going to shiver to death—as I started down the hallway. I vaguely remembered which room Kayla had said was hers. I heard a sound around the corner, where I couldn't see, and almost jumped out of my skin.

"Kayla?" I called hoarsely, my voice barely at a normal level. "Kayla?"

I knocked on her door, calling out her name.

There was no response.

I turned the knob and opened the door. The room was a mess, similar to the mess in my room, but this was just carelessness, not deliberate. I could see into the bathroom, and the black marble-topped vanity was a disaster area. There was a thin coat of powder on it, makeup containers scattered everywhere, and there was toothpaste spatter all over the sink and the mirror. It looked like Kayla just removed her clothes and let them fall wherever she happened to be standing at the time. Her bed was unmade, the coverlet lying next to the bed in a shapeless pile. Her phone was charging on the nightstand. Fashion magazines were tossed aside, some open on the bed, others fanned out on the carpet. Just looking at the mess made me cringe.

"Ariel?"

I'm not ashamed to admit I shrieked and jumped a bit. I spun around, trying to catch my breath. "You scared the crap out of me, Dustin!"

"I'm sorry." He was wearing black sweatpants and a ribbed red muscle shirt about a size too small. Black and gray hairs were escaping at the neckline, and his feet were bare. He was holding a toothbrush, and there was some white foam in the corners of his mouth. "I heard you calling Kayla. Is everything okay?"

I joined him in the hall, closing Kayla's door behind me, and gestured for him to follow me down the hall back to my room. He gasped when I opened the door and he saw the mess.

"I guess it's safe to assume this isn't how you left it?" he asked, folding his arms. The muscles in his shoulders and arms bulged. His voice was grim. "Is anything missing?"

I sat down on the bed, reaching down to pick up a couple of pairs of my underwear. Under normal circumstances I would be mortified to have a man—anyone—I barely knew see my undergarments scattered all over the floor. But this was hardly normal, and what Dustin thought about my underwear was the least of my concerns.

"The only thing of value in here that's mine is my laptop." I pointed to it on the nightstand. "I don't have jewelry that's worth anything. And they left the laptop." I stopped myself from mentioning the pictures being deleted from the computer and my cloud storage. I didn't know him well enough to trust him.

Okay, sure, he was a best-selling historian, and I'd seen him on television any number of times.

But he also had a room on the third floor. No one would question him going up the stairs to our floor, and he was the only other person staying up here. Both Kayla and I had been gone.

Could Kayla have done this?

Before we left for Lindsay's, I'd waited for both her and Bast downstairs. Both had been late, so it was entirely possible either of them could have gone to my room, deleted the pictures from my computer, and made the mess. I was calming down—thinking rationally always helped. Yes, it would have only taken a moment to open the drawers and throw everything around, take pants and sweaters and blouses from their hangers and toss them up in the air, strip off the bedclothes, and tip the mattress off the bed.

I could probably do this myself in maybe three minutes, tops. And my laptop was a MacBook—finding the pictures on it would have been a piece of cake.

Hollis was always warning me I needed to password-protect my laptop and set it to lock when not used. She was right, as always. I'd do that before I went to bed.

Although I wasn't sure I could sleep in this bed.

"I'm thinking it's not safe here," I heard Dustin saying. "First a murder, then the fire, and now this?" He gestured around the room with shaking hands. "I think I'm going to take the train back into the city in the morning. Do you want me to get help?"

"No, thank you." No, there was no point in calling the cops. Nothing had been taken. There was actually no reason for the mess, now that I thought about it more, other than it being a nuisance. Whoever had done this could have just accessed the pictures on my computer and deleted them, closed my laptop, and who knew how long it would have taken me to notice? I might have even thought I'd done it myself by accident—I'd done far stupider things on my laptop before. It could have been days before I'd noticed the pictures were gone. Whoever did this didn't know I hadn't deleted them from my phone after I'd copied them to my computer.

In fact, most people just uploaded their pictures directly to the cloud. I still did it the old-fashioned way, manually.

Someone was clearly worried about the pictures, so it stood to reason that whoever the figure was in the pictures with Angus was probably his killer.

Lindsay had thought it was Peggy.

Or had she been lying to me, trying to throw me off the trail? I couldn't tell who it was in the pictures. I wouldn't put anything past Lindsay. I didn't trust her.

Maybe she was working with the killer?

Maybe she *was* the killer.

But she couldn't have done this to my room, and anyway, I'd shown her the pictures, so she knew they were backed up.

Anyone, even someone with a very limited knowledge of computers and the internet would have assumed I'd backed the pictures up.

My stomach clenched.

Whoever had done this *wanted me to know they'd been in my room.*

I felt dinner turning in my stomach.

That was even more terrifying. This was a warning of some kind, a warning that the killer could get to me anytime he or she wanted to.

Dustin was right. Sea Oats wasn't safe for me anymore, either. The smart thing to do was lock the door tonight and take the train back into the city in the morning.

The killer was a member of the family, or someone close to them.

I got up from the bed and walked over to the bathroom, which was still pristine, the way the cleaning women had left it.

I turned on the sink and splashed cold water onto my face. Dustin was gone by the time I walked back out into the bedroom—probably back in his room packing, which was what I should be doing.

But as the shock and terror started fading away finally, I felt myself starting to get angry.

How dare someone get into my computer and throw my clothes around like this! The absolute contempt for me that showed.

Well, I was damned if I was going to be driven away from Sea Oats.

I walked back over to the hallway door and looked both ways. There was still no sign of life out there. All the doors I could see were closed. Kayla was probably downstairs with Bast in his room—she was keeping her clothes in another room in deference to Peggy, at Bast's insistence, but I doubted if Kayla would do more than pay lip service to the separate bedrooms thing.

I closed the door and turned back to face the mess. I started with picking up my scattered underwear, my hands still slightly shaking as I folded the items and put them back in the bureau drawer where they belonged. The thought of someone having their hands on them—I felt my gorge rising and I put my hand down on the bureau, lowered my head, and took some deep, cleansing breaths until my stomach subsided. Just the thought of someone touching my clothes, riffling through them…I seriously doubted I was going to be able to sleep well. How could I?

I did have those sleeping pills my doctor had given me,

but did I want to sleep that deeply? Wouldn't I be better off if I could wake up if I needed to?

I had finished with the underwear and had slipped the covers back onto the bed. By breaking it down to tasks—put the bed back together, pick up the clothes, then sort them, and put them away—I managed to stay focused and keep my mind under control, kept it from going to the dark, scared places it wanted to go. My hands were still shaking as I made the bed again, finding the pillows and covers in various corners of the room. I was just about to spread the coverlet back on it when there was a light knock on my door. "Come in," I called as I snapped the coverlet out and let it float down to the bed.

"Did Clarice not make your bed?" Peggy asked from the doorway in her *I'll have a chat with her the next time I see her and this won't happen again* voice.

"Someone searched my room," I replied grimly as I tucked the bedspread under the pillows. It was good enough like that, I decided, and started picking up the rest of my clothes. I started sorting them into piles, and Peggy joined me.

"But why?" Peggy asked, folding a pair of jeans. "Why would someone do this?"

I decided to be blunt. "The other day after running into you and Charlotte out by the maze, I took some pictures," I replied. "The way the colors were combining in the pre-storm light…Anyway, I just started clicking away with my phone, not really paying any attention. It turns out that I managed to get Angus in some of them."

"Angus? You mean—"

"Right before he was killed, yes." I nodded. "I didn't realize it at the time—it wasn't until I downloaded the pictures and started going through them I noticed he was there. And you can almost see—well, you can't really make out anything, but there's a bare glimpse of someone else, in the shadows cast by the maze. I can't tell who it is. And since it's likely Angus was killed shortly after I saw him…" I shrugged. "You do the math."

"Oh my God." She dropped the shirt she was folding and sat down hard on the bed. Her face had gone white. "You think—you think you took a picture of the killer?"

"Maybe. But whoever it is—if it is someone—you can't tell who it is. At least I can't. I'll be turning the pictures over to the police as soon as I can. Maybe there's something they can do with the pictures, enhance them somehow, I don't know, but maybe they can make it clearer."

"But why search your room?"

"Nothing's missing, at least that I can tell. But they went into my laptop and deleted the pictures." I folded my arms. I wasn't sure I could trust her, and not just because of Lindsay's accusation. She would do anything she could to protect Bast and Charlotte. I knew she would lie for them—but would she kill?

I hated not being able to trust Peggy, but she'd invited me to Sea Oats for her own reasons—first I'd thought as a pawn to break up Lindsay and Charlotte, then as a ploy to control the stock. But maybe there were other reasons she wanted me here.

"So the pictures are gone? I don't understand. How can you give them to the police if they've been deleted?"

There was no point in hiding the truth from her—Lindsay, Bast, and Kayla knew they were still on my phone. "I still have the originals on my phone."

"Oh, God." Peggy buried her face in her hands. "You need to get out of here. It's not safe for you here, Ariel. I'll get Joseph and have him drive you home tonight. You need to go."

"I'm not going anywhere," I said, more bravely than I felt. "Whoever did this wants me to go, Peggy. I'm staying."

"I'm afraid I have to insist—"

"I showed the pictures to Lindsay tonight." In for a penny, in for a pound. "She seemed to think it was you in the pictures with Angus."

"What?" Her face turned red. "She said that?"

I nodded. "I don't think she was serious. I mean, you really can't tell who it is, there's too much shadow, and the corner of the maze really is in the way. But why would she say such a thing?"

She tossed her arms up. "Who knows why Lindsay does anything she does, besides Lindsay?" She shook her head. "I've long since given up trying to figure her out, Ariel, and so has Charlotte. Why Char has started seeing her again is a mystery to me."

"Peggy, why am I here, really? Why did you send for me?"

"If I'd only known..." She shook her head. "All right. I'll tell you the truth. I owe you at least that much, for putting you in danger. I—"

"Yes, you do owe me," I replied. "I thought you wanted me and Char to get back together. But there's more, isn't there?"

She took a deep breath. "Ariel, I know Charlotte still loves you. If you both could just sit down and be honest with each other..."

"We will, Peggy, I promise you that. Even if it's just to work out how to handle the divorce."

"Don't say that." She winced. "Please don't say that, don't even think it."

"You have to know that divorce is on the table. I don't know if we can ever get back to what we once were, and you're deflecting, anyway. What is going on, Peggy?"

"You've probably picked up on some of the tension in the house." She made a face. "And you've probably heard something about what is causing it."

"Bast."

She nodded. "Yes. Bast. Bast did something extraordinarily stupid—"

"I've heard some of it. He borrowed a lot of money and lost it, is what I've gathered. But I don't understand why it's such a big deal. Why did he have to borrow money?"

"Oh, the stupid trusts." She grimaced. "You know both he and Charlotte only get a regular income from the trusts, and can't touch the principal unless both of them sign off on it, right?"

"Vaguely." I remembered Charlotte explaining it—or rather, trying to—when we were first married. "Charlotte lives on her salary and puts her income back into the trust."

"Yes. Well, Bast—even when he makes money, he goes through it very quickly." That was the most disloyal thing I'd ever heard her say about Bast. Usually, wild horses couldn't drag something negative or critical about Bast out of her. He could do no wrong in her eyes, or so I had thought. It was good to know her eyes weren't completely shut when it came to him.

"So he borrowed money and put up his shares of Swann's as collateral. Is that right?" I pursed my lips. "Charlotte wouldn't release the money from the trust?"

She raised an eyebrow. "That's part of it, yes. But it's a lot more complicated than you think. When Frank Swann created the trusts in the first place, there wasn't any intent in them being permanent. He was more concerned with the family money being divided up, as well as company ownership. He inherited the company and a fortune, of course, but he was worried it would just keep being divided and divided until no one owned a majority share of Swann's and the money had been divided so many times it didn't matter. Two years before Charlotte married you, she wanted to take the company public to raise some capital to pay some debts, get the company on solid footing, and invest back into the stores." She tilted her head to one side. "But to do that, she had to break the trust. It was easy enough to do, but it was a process. I don't understand completely how precisely it was done, but the majority of the company stock remained in the trust under Charlotte's and Bast's names, and they were able to issue enough stock so the trust remained the majority stockholder—so control remained within the family—but the trust was going to be dissolved. It was dissolved the summer you married Charlotte."

"And Charlotte didn't have me sign a prenup." I got up and walked over to the window. That was what Lindsay was hinting at. Since there was no prenuptial agreement in place, if we were to get divorced, I would have a claim on some of Charlotte's holdings.

And if there was a struggle for control of the business, every share mattered.

"Is that why Charlotte hasn't divorced me?" The last shred of hope I had that we might reconcile, that she might still have feelings for me, faded away. She hadn't divorced me because she was facing a proxy fight for control of Swann's. "I don't want anything from her. You can tell her that for me, Peggy. I got everything I wanted or needed from her when I left, and I can stand on my own now. I don't want anything from any of you."

"Charlotte hasn't divorced you because she still loves you," Peggy insisted. "She didn't know I invited you to come."

"You still haven't said why you did."

"I was hoping…I was hoping if you two were finally to come face-to-face you'd both get over your hurt pride and reconcile."

I sat down on the windowsill, my back to the window. "And weren't you a little afraid that the people who want to take over Swann's might come to me, try to get me on their side?"

"Would you do that to Charlotte?"

"I don't know." I didn't. I'd like to think I was mature enough that I wouldn't want revenge. But if I'd been properly approached…I pushed those thoughts out of my head. "Not now. I wouldn't now. But if someone had come to me after I went to New York, when I was still angry, I might have done something I'd regret now. And besides, this has everything to do with Bast, not me. If Bast hadn't been…" I let my voice trail off. Her face had started hardening the moment I mentioned his name.

No matter what he did, Bast would always be her little darling.

"You needn't worry, Peggy," I said, picking up the sweaters and putting them back in a drawer. The room looked more tidy now, although it needed vacuuming. But it didn't look like a tornado had swept through it anymore, and now I could handle staying in it.

One more night, at any rate.

Yes, police or no police, I was getting on the train and heading back into the city first thing in the morning. I'd had enough Swann drama. I'd turn the pictures over to the cops on my way to the train station. Once I was back in New York I'd get a lawyer and file for divorce. It would be simple. I didn't want anything from Charlotte or her family anymore. I just wanted to be left alone, forget all of them, forget that I was ever married.

Closure. I'd finally gotten some closure on the whole mess.

But…

I still had feelings for Charlotte, but I'd get over them in time. Her total lack of interest in me, and the way she'd successfully avoided me since that first accidental meeting out by the maze, told me everything I needed to know about how she felt about me. There wasn't a future here for me. There was nothing for me here anymore.

And the sooner I got back to the city, to my actual life, the better.

"I'll file for divorce as soon as I can find a lawyer," I went on. "But I don't want anything. Money, stock, I don't care. I just want to have my life back and pretend none of this ever happened."

"You love her still, don't you?" Peggy said. She stood up, smoothed the coverlet back. She always wanted everything perfect. "Don't lie to me, Ariel. I can see it in your face, hear it in your voice every time you say her name. Stay and fight for her."

"She doesn't feel the same, Peggy. She just sees me as a mistake she made. And I'm fine with it, Peggy. I am, really. I'm not sorry I came. I'm glad I saw her again, saw all of you again. I would have always wondered…"

I could feel myself starting to get emotional. I turned my back to her and looked out the window again.

"I wish I knew how to convince you that you're wrong." Peggy hugged me from behind, held on to my shoulders for a moment, and then I heard the door close behind her.

I leaned my head against the glass. There were lights on in the yard, so that it wasn't completely dark out there.

I wanted to believe her, oh, God, how I wanted to believe her! But I couldn't trust Peggy. She would do whatever she had to, say whatever she felt she needed, for Bast and Charlotte. If she thought lying to me about having a chance of working things out with my wife was the best thing for Charlotte, then she would say anything she could think of to get me to stay here. She'd admitted there was a concern about control of the company, a shareholder fight to come that sounded like it would be ugly and nasty.

But she hadn't said who was behind it. Lindsay hadn't either, nor had Kayla. No one seemed to know who it was. I wasn't sure how that was possible, but when it came to that sort of thing I didn't have any idea.

But Hollis, my boss, might.

I grabbed my phone and pulled up her number. The call went straight to voicemail. "Hollis, it's Ariel. I'm probably heading into the city tomorrow but I had a question I thought you could answer for me, about stocks and hostile takeovers. Can you call me if you get this"—I started to say *at a decent hour* but Hollis often was up until three in the morning—"before midnight. Thanks, call me on my cell. Hope all's well in my absence." I hung up, feeling only slightly idiotic.

I looked around the room again. With order restored, no one could tell what a mess I'd walked in on less than an hour earlier.

But who could have done this to my room?

I sat down on the windowsill again, looking out over the darkened lawn. I'd been so worried about the pictures being deleted, and my room being trashed, that I'd only thought about the killer. But who could have gotten into my room? It couldn't have been someone from the outside.

It had to have been someone staying at Sea Oats.

But who? Bast and Kayla had been with me at Lindsay's— although either one of them could have slipped into my room and tossed it while I was downstairs waiting for them, deleting the pictures from my laptop—

But if deleting the pictures was the reason for getting into my room, why had someone searched it and tossed it? Had someone been looking for something, or were they just sending me a message?

My reaction had been to plan an immediate return to the city.

Which was exactly what someone wanted me to do.

So the obvious answer was for me to stay, figure out what was going on around here, figure out who I could trust and who I couldn't.

I'd run away from Sea Oats once before. I wasn't going to do it again until it was on my own terms.

And if the Swanns sweated out whether I was going to want some shares in the company as part of my divorce settlement, well, I could use that fear to get Charlotte to sit down and talk to me, couldn't I?

A light flashed out on the lawn.

At first I thought I'd imagined it, since I only saw it out of the corner of my eye and I wasn't paying any attention, but then the light flashed again. It was a signal of some sort, like someone was using the flashlight app on their cell phone and covering the lens quickly with one hand. It came a third time. I could barely make out the figure standing out there on the lawn. The moon wasn't full and it was a cloudy night, so visibility was poor, but someone was definitely out there.

I carefully unlocked my window and slid it up, so the glass wasn't interfering with my ability to see. I squinted, then realized whoever it was could see me in the window. I walked over to the door and flipped the light switch. Other than the glow from my laptop screen, my room was completely dark now. I crept back over to the window and looked out again.

The lights on the gallery weren't on, so it was obvious when someone opened the front door to the house and went out; an enormous rectangle of light appeared on the driveway and someone's shadow—a shadow I couldn't make out—moved across it before the door shut again and the light was gone. I could see a figure moving quickly across the drive and through the trees and heading across the lawn, but again, I couldn't tell who it was.

I debated going out there, but I was up on the third floor and they could both be gone by the time I reached the front door.

The light flashed on the lawn again, and this time I could tell it was a woman out there, and it might have been my imagination but it looked like Lindsay.

Why would Lindsay be out there, and who would be going to meet her at this hour?

I glanced at my Fitbit and pressed the button. It was past eleven. The rest of the house was quiet, and most of the lights were out.

Maybe it was the same person who'd searched my room.

There was no need for either Charlotte or Peggy to search my room. That left Kayla, Bast, Roger, and Justin.

But Kayla and Bast hadn't been here when Angus was killed. And if the pictures were what they'd come into my room for, to get rid of potential evidence that would identify Angus's killer—that let Kayla and Bast out.

Could it have been Charlotte or Peggy? I couldn't believe Angus would ever do anything that would cause trouble for the Swanns; he'd been working for them so long that he seemed like part of the family, in that way rich people always said their staff were members of the family. But from what I remembered, he was devoted to them—except for Bast, whom he'd never forgiven for that trick he'd played with the maze as a teenager.

I shivered. Angus's killer had been right there with us both.

The center of the maze is where the truth lies. Those were his last words to me, trying to signal me that he was in danger, trying to tell me something in code, something he thought I'd understand, be able to pass along to someone else.

But it didn't make any sense to me. I'd always hated the maze, and Angus had known that I never wanted to go inside there.

So what did he mean?

The light flashed again. The woman—whoever she was—was leaving.

The person who'd met her out there was coming back to the house.

I watched until he disappeared out of sight, my view cut off by the gallery roof.

Chapter Ten

I was too keyed up to go to sleep without taking a sleeping pill—and I was too nervous to do that, so I decided to go back to my usual fallback: wine.

Wine never disappointed.

It took me longer than usual to go down the back staircase to the kitchen to get a bottle. I was nervous as a cat in a room full of rocking chairs. Every sound stood my hair on end, and I was constantly looking back over my shoulder to the point I almost missed a step once. If I hadn't had a firm hold of the railing I would have fallen all the way down to the first floor.

The kitchen was empty when I finally made it there. I flipped on the lights and headed for the wine refrigerator. I picked out a nice bottle of sauvignon blanc and was working on the cork when Charlotte said from behind me, "You know what they say about people who drink alone."

I almost dropped the bottle. "You really shouldn't sneak up on people like that. I could have dropped this bottle and what a waste would that have been?" I pulled on the corkscrew and the cork came out with a satisfying pop. I put the cork down on the counter and poured a glass before turning to look at her. "Then maybe you should join me, so I won't be drinking alone. I'd hate for people to talk about me."

She laughed. "Sure. Just don't poison me."

She looked tired. Her eyes were bloodshot, and the dark circles under her eyes were more pronounced than usual. Maybe it was a combination of being tired and stressed out. I wanted to take her in my arms, somehow make her feel like everything was going to be okay, but it wasn't my place anymore.

It was late for her to be up, now that I thought about it. She usually was up by five every morning for her commute into the office, and almost always tried to be in bed asleep by ten. That had been yet another one of our problems. She would come home late from the city, exhausted from her day, and just want to have dinner and go to bed. I'd spent my days lonely and bored, waiting for her at Sea Oats to come home. When she finally did get home, we would have dinner with the family, and when I finally had her all to myself, she was so tired all I would get from her would be one-syllable words in response. She never initiated conversations—and sex during the week was out of the question.

But my boredom hadn't been her fault. She hadn't asked me to quit my job, I'd done that on my own. And I didn't have to be so hard on myself, either. I'd worked all the way through college waiting tables at night, studying when I wasn't in class or at work, and barely averaging five hours of sleep per night. After interning with Hollis that last year, and then putting in ten to twelve hours a day when she'd hired me, I'd thought being a lady of leisure would be fun.

What it was, though, was boring. I wasn't cut out to be a housewife any more than Charlotte was. I couldn't remember when I'd had days to myself since high school. I'd even worked when I was in high school, cashiering at the McDonald's a couple of blocks from our house. At first, it was nice—sleeping late and not worrying about doing laundry or how the house was going to get cleaned or doing any grocery shopping. The first week had been lovely, but by the second week I felt like my mind was turning to mush.

I should have found a job, volunteered, done something, anything, to keep myself occupied during the days while she was at work. But young and bored and rebellious—and prodded, in no small part, by a troublemaking Bast—I blamed everything on Charlotte. She didn't have time for me, she didn't pay enough attention to me, whine, whine, whine.

Just thinking about it made me wince inwardly. It was a wonder she hadn't asked me to leave. But she hadn't. She'd put up with my tantrums and my pouting and my bullshit, tolerated it, tried to help me find something to fill my days. Her rational responses to my emotional outbursts only fanned the flames of my immaturity. "Why didn't you tell me to get a job when I lived here?" I handed her the glass and put the bottle down on the table.

She toasted me with the glass and took a drink. She grinned at me. "Excellent taste, Ariel, that's a good wine." She put the glass down and looked at me. "I should have, you know. I did a lot of things wrong."

I clinked my glass against hers. "You're not the only one," I replied. "I knew how hard you worked when I married you. I shouldn't have expected, or wanted, that to change after we got married."

"You've done really well since you went back to work for Hollis," she observed. "I was proud of you when I saw that piece in the *Times*."

Butterflies started fluttering in my stomach, and I could feel my face redden at her praise. "Thank you," I managed to get out, taking another drink to hide my embarrassment. "Peggy told me what's going on with Swann's. I'm sorry, Charlotte. I know how much the company means to you."

Her face tightened. "Control of the company will be taken away from me when they pry it out of my cold dead hands," she said grimly. "Bast was a fool. I warned him about that investment." She shook her head. "It stank to high heaven, and if I'd known he'd be fool enough to put his stock up as collateral..." Her voice trailed off. "It would have been better had he lost the money from the trust than this."

"If you're worried about me causing trouble, don't be."

She laughed, brushing a lock of reddish-gold hair from her forehead. "So this is what our marriage has come to, is it?" She locked her eyes on mine. "I knew I never had to worry about you, Ariel. No matter what is going on between us, I knew you'd never side with outsiders against the family."

"You don't have any idea who's behind the takeover?"

"All we know is a holding company called Malone Holdings is buying up our stock. They're incorporated in the Caymans, so..." She shrugged. "But I've got people on it, Ariel. No need for you to worry about it."

"Malone? Where have I heard that name lately?" I took another drink of the wine. It was excellent—but there was never bad wine at Sea Oats. "Oh, yes, Dustin mentioned it to me. Some maid one of Arabella's sons got pregnant—Arabella bought her off and sent her away."

"Brigid Malone?" Charlotte laughed. "You can't be serious? I'm sure that's just a coincidence."

"Don't be so sure," I replied, trying to not get upset and not entirely succeeding. "It's a possibility."

"You think one of Brigid Malone's descendants is trying to punish the family for old misdeeds?" She laughed again. "I'd forgotten what a fan of melodrama you are."

"It wouldn't hurt to track her descendants down," I pointed out, keeping my voice level, trying not to let her see how insulting she was being again.

"Oh, don't get your feelings hurt. I didn't mean anything by it."

Same old Charlotte—always so dismissive of my feelings and opinions! Some things never changed. "My feelings aren't hurt."

"I know that look on your face. I've seen it before."

"Well, enjoy it while you can. I'm leaving in the morning." I resisted the urge to add, *and finding a lawyer as soon as I can.*

It wouldn't accomplish anything.

"It's probably for the best, all things considered. Peggy said your room was searched?" She frowned, her eyebrows meeting over her nose.

"Yeah." I took another big gulp of wine, not wanting to say anything else because I was afraid I might start shaking again. I wasn't going to give her that satisfaction.

"Lock your door tonight," she said. "I've asked one of the guards to stay in the house tonight, make sure everyone's safe. I'm sorry that happened."

"No kidding." I shivered. "I have to say I never thought I'd ever feel unsafe at Sea Oats but now…" I took my phone out of my pocket and opened the photo app, scrolled through till I found the pictures of Angus, and passed it across the table to her. "You can't really see anything in the pictures, but I'm going to stop by the police station on my way into the city tomorrow. I guess they can maybe enhance them somehow, clear up the blurring and shadows, maybe identify whoever that is."

She squinted at the screen for a couple of moments, then scrolled to the next. I finished my wine while she went through the pictures and refilled the glass. I topped off hers, noting that she didn't stop me. She usually didn't drink on work nights, either. Alcohol always made her groggy the next morning, and it didn't take much for her to have a hangover.

Maybe she needed wine to deal with me.

She finally handed the phone back to me. "I can't tell who that is, if it's even a person or just some weird effect from the camera," she admitted, tiredly pushing the errant lock of hair away from her forehead again. "I'm still having trouble wrapping my mind around the idea that someone killed poor old Angus." She cracked another smile. "I mean, if anyone around here was going to be killed, my money would have been on Bast."

"Mine, too." I hesitated. "Speaking of Bast, Charlotte…I just want you to know you don't have to worry about me and a divorce—I don't want anything from you, so if the stock is an issue for you, or if you're worried about that, you don't have to be. I don't want anything from you." My voice was shaking, so I gripped the arms of my chair.

"So you do want a divorce?" She stiffened a bit, but then relaxed.

"Don't you?" I replied. "You made it clear to me you didn't trust me two years ago, and if you don't trust me, there's really not any point in staying married anymore, is there?" *Why didn't you come after me?* I wanted to scream the words at her, but that wouldn't be fair to either one of us. It was over.

She picked up her glass. "I don't know what I want anymore." Her voice was bitter. "With everything going on at Swann's, do you mind waiting a while longer? I know it's a lot to ask, but I just can't deal with anything else right now."

She is worried about you wanting some of her stock, despite her protestations to the contrary, a little voice whispered inside my head, and it sounded like Lindsay Moore's. *Don't fool yourself into thinking it's anything else.*

I exhaled. "It won't hurt me to wait a little longer." Part of me wanted to beg her to take me back, to tell her I would do anything she wanted me to for this to all work out. But I shut that down. I wasn't going to humiliate myself in front of her any more than I already had. "But we can't go on forever like this."

"Are you seeing someone?"

She wasn't looking at me, her eyes focused on her wine. At first I was touched that she cared, that she wanted to know, but then I remembered she was seeing Lindsay again. She was just making polite conversation with me, but this…this was better than us not being able to be in the same room together, wasn't it?

"No," I replied finally. "I've been too busy, focusing on my work."

"That really was a great piece in the *Times*." She was still staring into her wine like she could see the future in the golden liquid. "I was proud of you, Ariel. You're making a name for yourself."

"It's nice to have my hard work pay off." It was like we were total strangers talking, chatting about careers and work and things, like we'd never been intimate, shared a bed and a life and plans for the future together. "Hollis has more or less promised to make me a full partner later this year. I do like working." I laughed. "Maybe if I hadn't—oh, at this point there's not really any point to Monday-morning quarterbacking, is there?"

"Maybe…" She hesitated, still not looking up. "Maybe you'll have another client fall for you."

I laughed. "Yeah, probably not my most professional moment. I was terrified that would be in the article."

Redecorating the executive offices of Swann's had been my first big job as lead designer. I'd been working for Hollis Allman since I graduated after interning for her while I was in college. An associate designer at Hollis's firm was only slightly higher than an intern on the food chain. I didn't get to contribute much to any of the work the lead designers were doing on any project I was assigned to; many times I bounced from one job to another before they were finished. I got coffee, made sure supplies were ordered and paint was available, rode herd on contractors, made copies, and was pretty much required to keep track of multiple different projects at one time. I also got some small jobs—apartments or houses too small for the attentions of the more experienced designers—and I was proud of those jobs. I'd just redone a small apartment for the daughter of one of Hollis's friends from her college days, and that was the key to getting the gig from Swann's. But first I had to land the account. That was the real test; if I was able to sell Charlotte Swann on my designs and our firm, that would be a big step up the ladder to being a lead designer—and eventually, as my original career plan had run, own my own firm.

I'll never forget that first meeting with Charlotte. It was an interview, really, with me bringing my portfolio with me. I'd been in Swann's before—their flagship store in Manhattan might not be as iconic as Macy's on Thirty-Fourth Street, but it was pretty famous. I loved shopping there. When I was young, I'd dreamed of leaving the Midwest for New York as a career woman, and shopping at Swann's, like the heroine of countless movies from the fifties.

There was just something about getting off the subway that day and walking the couple of blocks into Swann's that made me feel—and I knew how silly this seemed—like an adult. Riding the elevator up past the shopping floors to the executive suites, in my black pantsuit, my portfolio under my arm, imagining I was Doris Day in *Pillow Talk* on my way to meet a prospective client—now it seemed silly and immature. Waiting in the outer office while Charlotte's secretary pounded away at her keyboard and answered the phones while I waited, looking around at the heavy dark wooden paneling, the worn carpet, the heavy oil paintings of former Swanns who'd run the company, I felt my nerves starting to jangle and butterflies fluttering in my stomach. This was a big job, and it was a big deal that Hollis was letting me handle it. If I landed this job, I might even wind up with my own private office instead of a cubicle in the big workroom.

The big wooden door opened behind the secretary's desk and out came Charlotte Swann. I'd done my research on her, of course—anyone doing a pitch without doing research didn't have a chance of getting the job. Charlotte Swann was already legendary in the business world. Her parents had died when she was young, and the company had been run for the family until she graduated from Penn with an MBA from Wharton School of Business. She'd then spent a year studying the business, learning how the company was run, traveling the world and visiting every store in the chain, sizing them up for herself, and getting to know the team. Then she took over as CEO of Swann's, and under her direction, Swann's not only never had a downturn no matter what happened with the economy and survived the onslaught of online shopping and other changes in the market, but grew. Anytime she was forced to close a store, she took care of the employees or found them other jobs within the company—Swann's employees were made to feel by management like they mattered and were important, and thus were incredibly loyal to the company. She got rid of lines that weren't selling and brought in brands that would sell. She took Swann's public—at least partly public—in order to get some capital to launch some new initiatives as well as to make the company more sound financially. I'd researched the big house out on Long Island the Swanns called home, looked up pictures of the house's interior, looked at the stores themselves.

I'd seen pictures of Charlotte, usually with other people

at business gatherings or charity events, but she was much more attractive in person. Photographs couldn't capture her vitality and so never did her justice. She'd never been linked romantically to anyone in the press—I'd found out about Lindsay later—and she was in her midthirties, so she was either a lesbian or really good at keeping her private life private.

She led me into her office after a handshake and a friendly greeting. "Thank you for coming to meet with me," she said after I declined her offer of something to drink. "As you can see, the office hasn't been redecorated since the Coolidge administration." Her office was very masculine in style, with dark heavy furniture, an enormous desk, and heavy brocade curtains. "You can still smell the cigarette smoke, can't you?" She sat down behind her desk. "I've wanted to have all the offices redecorated since I took over the company, but this is the first chance I've had. What do you have for me?"

I spread out my portfolio on her desk, which was pristine. "Are you looking for something more modern?" I asked.

I was only supposed to be there for half an hour, but I wound up talking to Charlotte and brainstorming ideas with her for a good two hours. I couldn't believe so much time had passed when her secretary buzzed her to let her know her four o'clock appointment was there.

It goes without saying that I got the job.

It was one of the easiest jobs I've ever had. Charlotte was the best client—she asked the right questions, didn't get in the way, and unlike so many other clients, she didn't want anything cheap or any corners cut. Sometimes when I was there, working, I'd catch her watching me, and other times I would catch myself stealing glances at her. I'd never met another woman like her, and I was attracted to her, much as I hated to admit it. One of Hollis's strictest rules was no fraternization with clients, and much as I liked Charlotte Swann, much as I was attracted to her, much as I dreamed about her when I was at home at night in my bed unable to sleep, I would never cross that line with a client, no matter how badly I wanted to.

"So, that's everything," I said on the last day. The paint was dry, the wallpaper up, the new carpet laid. I'd already taken hundreds of photographs of the job—it was definitely going into my portfolio. Everything gleamed, the mix of modern with the classic old styles merging synchronously to create a whole new look for the offices. I put the final tabulation of the outstanding bill down on her desk and slid it across to her.

She pursed her lips, slid her glasses on, and went over every line of the bill. Finally, she set it down and whistled. "You did an excellent job, Ariel. You did exactly what I wanted, what I was looking for. Are you a mind reader?"

I'd smiled back at her. "No, but anticipating a client's needs and wants is something every good designer should be able to do."

She pulled an enormous checkbook out of one of her desk drawers and wrote out a check for the full amount, made a notation on the stub, and tore it out, pushing it across the desk to me. "And so this concludes our business?"

I put the check into my purse and smiled back at her. "Yes, it does."

"So in that case Hollis wouldn't be offended if you were to join me for dinner this evening."

"Hollis," I replied with a big smile, "has no say in this whatsoever."

And here we were, almost three years later, sitting around the kitchen table at Sea Oats drinking white wine and dancing around the elephant in the room.

"Hollis should just go ahead and make you a full partner right now," Charlotte was saying as she refilled her glass. She was going to have a really thick head in the morning.

"Should you be having so much wine on a work night?" I teased. "As for full partner, I agree with you, but Hollis does things her own way. And I'm fine with it. I'm making good money, and as you noted, my reputation is growing."

"She'll need to make you a partner to keep you from going out on your own." She hesitated. "Do you think if you'd not given up your career, things might have worked out differently between us?"

I blinked a few times. She'd said it so casually. Her face was always unreadable, but I wished I could have gotten some sense of where she was going with this before I answered. "Maybe," I replied slowly. "Who's to say? Maybe things would have been different if we'd gotten married a week later, or a day sooner, or…that's just how things go." I felt myself getting emotional, and I was damned if that was going to happen in front of her. I finished my glass and got up. "I think it's past time for me to go to bed."

"I'm sorry," she said softly when I reached the door to the back stairs.

"Don't be," I said, not turning around.

"Can we talk more tomorrow, before you leave?" She was behind me, her hands on my shoulders. "I've been so tied up, worried about the company—I always put the company first, I'm sorry, but we just need to sit down together and talk. I'm not going into the city tomorrow, so maybe…maybe we could take a walk along the beach the way we used to, before you go?"

I nodded, and pushed through the door and headed up the stairs, blinking back tears. Every Saturday morning when I'd lived here we'd gone for a long walk along the beach after breakfast. Even when I felt like we'd grown so far apart nothing could bring us back together, those walks had been so wonderful, meant so much to me, always gave me the hope we'd be able to work anything, everything, out.

Don't get your hopes up, don't get your hopes up, I repeated to myself as I tried to hold the tears back as I climbed the stairs. *It's over, you knew that before you came back here, of course she still has feelings for you...but she doesn't love you anymore.*

Despite my best efforts I was crying by the time I got back to my room, making sure to lock the door behind me. I stared at the mirror and let myself go, giving in to the tears I'd never allowed myself to cry before about the failure of my marriage, about the death of our love for each other. I don't know how long I was in the bathroom, but finally I was cried out, drained and exhausted and ready for bed. I washed my face, brushed my teeth, and changed into my jersey. I slipped under the covers, staring at the ceiling as the wind whipped around the house.

It wasn't a surprise that I couldn't sleep. I tossed and turned, tried keeping my eyes closed, wondering if I was in fact asleep and just dreaming I was awake, opening my eyes to check—and of course, finding out that I was wide awake. The luminous digital numbers on the alarm clock on the nightstand changed slowly from 12:30 to 12:37 to 12:42.

But my mind couldn't stop remembering better times with Charlotte. Like the night she proposed, how she'd held me that first time I came here, and how thrilled she was that there were swans on the pond, excitedly telling me what a good omen that was, that it showed that we were meant to be.

So much for *that* sign, right? Just went to show how you couldn't put stock in things like that.

It was kind of inevitable that I would be bombarded with memories while I lay there trying to sleep. I figured it was kind of like how they say your life flashes before your eyes just before you die, only it was my marriage flashing before my eyes before it died. The honeymoon in Italy, the gondola ride in Venice, the trip through the Uffizi Gallery in Florence, the Coliseum in Rome. I'd always dreamed of going to Italy, and this had been the perfect trip—

I heard a noise out in the hallway.

I sat up in the bed, immediately aware, reaching for something I could use as a weapon if needed. I strained to hear, but there was nothing else.

I had just about decided it had been just my imagination when I heard the noise again.

I picked up my phone. I didn't turn on my nightstand light—if someone was actually out there I didn't want them to know I knew they were there. I crept over to my door. I unlocked it and eased it open as slowly as I could, hoping that the hinges didn't squeak or give me away. The hallway lights were still on, and I heard it again, only this time it was coming from around the corner of the hallway, close to where Dustin's room was.

Maybe it was just the guard Char had said would be patrolling the house.

My heart was pounding.

I took a deep breath and crept down the hallway, my bare feet making no noise on the carpet. When I reached the corner, I peeked around it.

The door to the staircase to the attic was open, and the light was on.

Obviously, I should have gone and gotten someone, like maybe the guard, but it didn't occur to me at the time. All I thought was, *Why is that door open, nobody should be up in the attic at this hour*, and like an idiot, I walked over and looked up the staircase. The lights were on, and I heard another noise up there where no one should be.

Like the stupid heroine in every horror movie ever, I started climbing the stairs slowly. "Hello?" I called out. "Who's up there? The guard's on his way."

I added that last bit so I wouldn't feel quite as stupid.

There was no answer, but I kept going.

All I was missing were the damned high heels.

I was about halfway up the stairs when a blast of wind came tearing down the stairs and the door at the bottom blew shut.

I knew what that meant.

Someone had gone out onto the roof.

"Go get help," I muttered to myself but oh, no, like an idiot I kept going up the stairs. When I reached the top, the attic lights were also on. The wind felt damp, like it was going to rain again, but that door—I had to see who'd gone out onto the roof. "Hello?" I called again as I walked across the attic.

I paused at the door to the widow's walk. It was dark out there, and I'd never been a fan of heights. I'd only been up to the roof once. The widow's walk was flat and had a wrought-iron railing, about three feet high. The rest of the roof was slanted and it was a long way to the ground.

Charlotte had brought me up here once, to show me what a great view of the grounds and the sea there was from the widow's walk. The view had indeed been terrific, but I hadn't been comfortable out there.

"Hello?" I called again, stepping through the doorway and out onto the dark widow's walk.

I didn't see who it was but I heard them coming at me, and before I could turn or say anything I was lifted in the air and shoved over the railing.

I hit the slanted side of the roof with a thud and I screamed.

I heard running footsteps and the slamming of the attic door as I started sliding down the shingles.

My heart was thudding.

So this is it. I am going to die.

My skin was being torn and shredded by the weather-worn tiles as I slid. I scrabbled with my hands, desperately trying to grab a hold of something, anything that would keep me from going over the side.

My feet hit the gutter and it gave beneath me, and I went over the side.

CHAPTER ELEVEN

I've always been afraid of heights.

My earliest childhood memory was of me being taken on a Ferris wheel ride at the county fair or an amusement park when I was very small. I was absolutely terrified the entire time, so terrified that I couldn't cry or scream or anything because I was certain if I did anything at all the gondola would tip or flip and send me plunging to my death. After that I had a recurring nightmare. In it, I was bouncing on a trampoline like we did in my gym classes at school, doing seat drops and barrel rolls and flips, but in my dream I just kept sailing up in the air, getting higher and higher until I was bouncing so high that the trampoline looked like a postage stamp far below me and I knew I'd bounced too high and then I hung there for just a moment, weightless, knowing I'd gone too high and would die when I got back down, my weight crashing through the trampoline netting and all of my bones shattering against the gymnasium floor. I always woke up just as I started falling back to the trampoline surface, panting and sweating and my heart thumping in my ears. It always took a long time for me to go back to sleep after the nightmare. I avoided roller coasters, never looked down the sides of buildings from windows, hated driving in the mountains.

A trip to the observation deck of the Sears Tower when I was a kid gave me nightmares for weeks afterward.

I refused to go to the observation deck of the Empire State Building, or up inside the Statue of Liberty. One time on a work trip to Washington I'd gotten vertigo going down the massive escalator to the Dupont Circle Metro stop.

So as my worst nightmare became real and I went over the edge of the roof, my life didn't flash before my eyes, nor did everything seem to be happening in slow motion or any of the other clichés.

It happened so fast.

One moment I was scrabbling, tearing the skin on my hands and fingers while trying to get a grip on something, anything, to keep me from going over the edge of the roof—and then there was nothing beneath me but air. My legs were over the edge, nothing beneath them, and *I am going to die* was all that flashed through my mind as my legs swung out before the rest of my body went over the side.

It didn't seem like I hung there for that brief moment like they always do in movies and cartoons, either. No, one moment I was on the roof and the next I was falling through the air. It happened so fast I didn't even have time to scream.

In the next second I landed, hard, on one of the balcony roofs on the second floor, falling maybe thirteen feet in total. All the air was knocked out of me when I hit the roof and there was a definite cracking sound. I lay there, trying to get my breath back, in shock, still not comprehending what happened to me, staring up at a cloud-covered dark sky, my heart pounding in absolute terror as my mind finally started functioning again.

Oh my God someone just threw me off the roof someone just tried to kill me oh my God how lucky I was to fall onto a balcony a few feet in either direction and I would be dead oh my God oh my God oh my God.

I managed somehow to finally catch my breath, but started hyperventilating almost immediately, and there was a roaring in my ears and it seemed like all the edges of my vision were going dark and my sight was narrowed down to a thin tunnel and I was shaking my whole body was shaking and shivering and trembling and through it all I could feel pain, somewhere something was hurting but I still couldn't make any sound, I tried to catch my breath again to stop hyperventilating but I couldn't remember what I was supposed to do to stop it and then I heard another crack and this time realized it was beneath me.

It was the roof. It wasn't going to hold.

The cracking sound I'd heard when I landed was the wooden roof of the balcony.

There was another crack, and the roof shifted underneath me.

Oh my God oh my God I'm going to fall again.

I opened my mouth and screamed.

But once I was out of breath there was another shift, and I knew I had to get off the balcony roof. I was still not able to think as clearly as I would have liked, but if the balcony was on the second floor there was a chance that crashing through it would cause me to break through the balcony itself—and some of the balconies at Sea Oats had furniture on them. I still didn't know if I'd broken any bones yet—I was still in enough shock that I wasn't feeling any pain—but I had to get off the roof. If I didn't get off the roof it was going to collapse beneath me and I was going to fall again and—

Maybe if I got off before it collapsed…

It seemed rational at the time. I wasn't sure how injured I

was, but my body was racing with adrenaline, and I just knew, *knew*, that I had to get off that roof or I was going to die.

I couldn't hear anything, couldn't tell if anyone was coming to my rescue, to help me. I was on my own.

I was going to have to save myself.

I rolled over onto my side and winced at the stabbing pains I felt in my ribs, but I could still breathe, so I doubted that any of them were broken, so that was good, right, my injuries wouldn't stop me from getting down.

I flexed my arms and my legs, moved my feet and hands.

Nothing seemed to be broken.

But it was like thinking about not hurting was license for my body to start aching, and my back was screaming bloody murder, and so was one of my shoulders, and my head, come to think of it, my head was throbbing, too.

I took a deep breath and willed myself to look—and I looked over the side.

I gasped.

The lawn looked very far down. It was like my dream about the trampoline, and I sobbed, could feel the tears running down my face.

You have to do this, Ariel, you have to get down from here and you don't have much time, you don't have a choice, you can do it. You can do it, Ariel.

There was another loud crack and again, the roof shifted, and I felt myself sink down another few inches.

I didn't have much time to dither. If I didn't do something—

I closed my eyes and whispered to myself, *You can do it.*

I flipped my legs around, toward the edge.

You can do it, you can do it, you can do it.

I took a deep breath and rolled over onto my stomach. My back and shoulder screamed again, but I gritted my teeth and grabbed onto a broken piece of wood. I screamed again as a splinter from the board stabbed through my left palm, but I also managed to get my legs over the side.

They dangled there and I held on to that board as hard as I could.

I felt for the balcony railing with my bare feet.

I couldn't remember how far above the balcony the roof was.

Whimpering a little, repeating, *You can do this*, over and over again inside my head, I lowered myself a little farther. The wind was picking up, and I was shivering.

What if I missed the railing what if the angle was wrong what if I let go and just—

My left foot touched wood.

My right foot was still swinging in the air, but then it connected with the railing. Now both feet were on it...I just hoped it could hold my weight.

An image of the railing breaking away and falling into the void flashed through my head.

Stop that, I commanded myself.

Now all I had to do was figure out what to do next. Both feet might be shaking but they were on the railing, however solid it might be. Should I let go of the side of the balcony roof? Should I start swinging, and when I had enough momentum let it carry me down to the balcony?

Or would I fall just like in my nightmares?

But I couldn't let go. I told myself to let go, commanded my hands to let go, tried to balance.

But nothing happened. I kept hanging on, even though my shoulder was aching, my back was aflame with pain, my head was pounding, and the splinter in my palm hurt like a son of a bitch.

I couldn't make myself let go.

It seemed in my head to be easy. Let go of the roof, keep

your balance with one hand, bend at the knees, and fall forward onto the balcony itself.

But my hands wouldn't release the side of the roof.

You have to let go, I said to myself, *or you'll be out here all night or until the roof collapses and wouldn't that be the stupidest thing ever, to survive being thrown off the roof but getting killed because you were too afraid to let go of the balcony roof? You're an idiot, you can do this, let it go.*

My hands were still holding on.

Maybe someone would come rescue me? But who?

I couldn't get the image of myself falling backward off the railing out of my head.

I bit my lip and willed myself to let go with my left hand.

Sweat trickled down into my left eye. But my hand opened, the movement jarring the splinter, and I screamed again.

"I've got you!" someone shouted from below, and I felt someone grabbing me around the waist. I didn't have a choice about letting go—whoever grabbed me pulled me down so hard my right hand lost its grip on the roof and I felt myself falling.

And I screamed again.

But I somehow thought to make my body go limp as I fell, and my body crashed into someone, whoever it was who'd grabbed me and pulled me down, and we crashed down to the floor of the balcony.

Still, I saw the floor of the balcony coming right at my head and then everything went dark.

"Ariel! Can you hear me?"

It was Charlotte's voice penetrating the fog inside my head. I opened my eyes and they couldn't focus, everything was a blur, a kaleidoscope of colors mixing together as they spun around and around until my stomach felt like it was going to cramp up. My head ached, and all I was aware of was this throbbing pain in my head that pushed aside everything, any attempt at thought. It felt like someone was hitting my brain with a hammer at five-second intervals, and I would have sold my soul or jumped off the roof on my own to make it stop.

"Can you sit up?" Charlotte again, her voice somehow getting through the agony in my head.

I tried to sit up, hands grabbing me on both sides and I winced again, the splinter in my palm then my ribs and my back and my shoulder all competing with my head for attention, my whole body aching somehow. I moaned and realized that I was in the suite of rooms I used to share with her, which meant I was in the bed we'd shared. The hands helped me to sit up and I opened my eyes again, the colors starting to take shape now in spite of the pain, the pain, everywhere hurt, everything hurt. What was wrong with me? And I knew I had to get out of there, and I didn't belong in the bed I used to share with Charlotte, and I wanted out of there immediately, but even as I tried to get out of the bed hands were gently pushing me back down. I didn't resist, instead letting my eyes close and letting my aching body go limp.

I couldn't remember any other time when my entire body ached the way it did at that moment.

"Is she passing out again?" That was Peggy, her voice hushed and anxious. "Should I call for an ambulance?"

"No, I'm not," I managed to croak out. I opened my eyes a slit and glanced around. Charlotte was kneeling next to the bed on my right, Peggy was on the other side, and it looked like Kayla at the foot of the bed. No one else in the house, though, would have worn a baby doll nightgown, so it had to be her. "I just—I hurt everywhere."

"Can you move your legs?" This was Charlotte, her voice

calm but slightly shaky. I obliged her question by moving them, and moving my arms and turning my head from side to side as well.

"I'm fine, I just hurt everywhere."

"Does it hurt to breathe?" This was Kayla, excited and curious, but concerned, too. "A friend of mine broke a rib on a shoot, and it hurt her to breathe."

I took a few deep, slow breaths. It ached a little but it wasn't so bad.

"We need to take her to the hospital," Charlotte said. "Just to be on the safe side. You could have a concussion—you hit your head pretty hard."

"Yes, fine." I hated going to the doctor, hated hospitals, but I knew she was right. And if one of my ribs was broken—well, better to find out sooner rather than later. "But can I just rest here a little bit first?"

"What in the name of God were you doing up on the balcony roof? How did you get there?" Charlotte's tone was sharp and angry. Now that she didn't have to worry, she'd moved on to anger, like always.

Some things never changed.

I opened my eyes. "I couldn't sleep, and then I heard a weird noise in the hall, and when I went to look, the door to the attic stairs was open, which I thought was strange so I went to check it out. When I got up to the attic, the door out to the widow's walk was open. When I went out there, someone pushed me off the roof."

The room went completely silent.

Through the pain, I realized again: someone tried to kill me.

"Are you crazy? Why didn't you go get help before you went up there?" Charlotte exploded. "After everything that's happened? Why didn't you go get the guard?"

"I—well, I wasn't thinking clearly, obviously," I replied hotly. "I didn't think—I didn't think anyone wanted to hurt me. Trust me, I won't make that mistake again."

"You need to be checked out by a doctor," Peggy said into the silence that followed. "Should I call for an ambulance?"

"I don't need an ambulance," I said, shifting in the bed. My head was hurting and I ached everywhere, but nothing seemed to be broken. "If someone can drive me to the emergency room, I would appreciate that…maybe have some X-rays done? My head hurts really bad."

Charlotte's tone changed. "Are you all right?"

"She might have a concussion." That was Peggy, her voice hushed.

"I think I'm okay, but my head hurts and I ache all over and I'm scraped up and I want to make sure I'm okay, maybe get some painkillers so I can think clearly." My tone was sharper than I'd intended, and so I added, "I hit my head. It's not a bad idea to get that checked out. But I don't want or need an ambulance, just someone to drive me." I started to get up but got a bit dizzy and had to sit back down.

Charlotte and Peggy rushed to my side and helped me get up, holding on to me until the dizziness passed. Peggy got my jacket, and they helped me down the stairs, Kayla galloping along in front of them.

When Charlotte went to get her car, I asked, "Kayla, didn't you hear anything?"

She shook her head. "I took a sleeping pill. I have insomnia." She yawned. "I woke up when I heard you screaming. I probably won't be able to fall back asleep." She made it sound like it was my fault, but maybe I was being a little too sensitive.

The headlights of Charlotte's maroon MG swung around to the front of the house, and Peggy helped me down the front stairs. It wasn't until I was seat-belted into the passenger seat that I wondered where Bast was.

Had Bast been the one to lure me out on the roof, intent on killing me?

But why would *Bast* want me dead?

It didn't make any sense. Why would anyone want me dead? The pictures I took—no one could tell who that was in them, if it even was someone, and I hadn't seen anyone when I was out there the day Angus died. There was nothing I could tell the police, so why come after me?

Unless there was a personal reason for someone to want me dead.

Much as I disliked her, I couldn't see Lindsay trying to kill me to get me out of the picture. Besides, how would she have gotten into the house and up in the attic?

Then again, I'd seen her on the grounds. If the security guards were locals, they would know her and wouldn't think anything of letting her on the grounds or in the house. It seemed like an open secret that she and Charlotte were seeing each other again.

But surely she wouldn't go that far? I'd told her I was getting a divorce, so the path to what she'd always wanted was open.

She didn't need to kill me to get me out of the way.

It didn't make any sense.

I would make a terrible detective.

I slumped down in my seat.

"Are you all right?" Charlotte asked, glancing over at me as we waited for the gates to open. "Are you sure we shouldn't have called an ambulance?"

"I don't need an ambulance, Charlotte," I replied testily. "I'm just really tired and achy and sore, and realizing that someone tried to kill me tonight—you know, that's not a great feeling. I was almost killed." I repeated the last sentence again and started shivering.

She reached behind the seat and gave me a blanket, which I gratefully wrapped around my body. I was probably going into shock yet again, and my teeth were chattering. She turned the heater up, redirected the vents so they were blowing on me.

She didn't speak until she was driving through the gates. "You really think someone tried to kill you?"

"Charlotte, my head hurts, but are you suggesting that I went up there and jumped?" I bit my lip and counted to ten before continuing. "Someone lured me up to the roof and pushed me off, Char," I finally said, managing somehow to keep my voice level and even. "I was stupid to go up there instead of getting help, but someone pushed me, Charlotte. I can still feel their hands on my back." I began shaking again as I remembered how it felt as my body went over the widow's walk railing, sliding down the slanted roof, that horrible weightless feeling as I went over the edge and fell through space.

"I'm sorry, okay?" She kept her eyes on the road as she accelerated toward Penobscot. "I...I don't want to think about that, I don't want to think things have gotten so bad that someone would try to kill you—"

"Someone killed Angus," I reminded her, my eyes still closed, "and set your office on fire. I didn't make that up, either, remember? Are you going to finally tell me what the hell is going on at Sea Oats? Now that I've almost been killed?"

She sighed tiredly. "You really picked the worst possible time to come back here," she said, gripping the steering wheel so tightly her knuckles whitened. "So many other times in the last two years you could have called, or come back, or stopped by my office...Why now, Ariel?"

My head was hurting still. "The phone works two ways. And you knew you could reach me through my office, too. Why didn't you reach out to me, Char? Do you still believe—you couldn't have believed that Bast and I..."

She stiffened. "Bast is a good-looking man, and women have been throwing themselves at him for as long as I can remember."

"For God's sake, I'm a *lesbian*, Charlotte." I closed my eyes and rested my aching head against the car window. My voice sounded more tired than angry. I just didn't care anymore. "I've *never* been with a man. I've never had any desire to be with a man. My parents don't even speak to me anymore because I'm a lesbian. My whole family has cut me off because I like women, Charlotte. And yet despite all of that, somehow you are still so willing to believe that Bast—your brother—is so unbelievably hot and sexy that I would change everything about my life, the way I feel, the way I am wired somehow, and go straight? Just for him? I don't know whether to be offended or angry or hurt, to be honest. And while I am saying my piece, finally, can I just add—how very dare you, Charlotte?"

I could feel tears forming behind my eyelids. I'd always known I was a lesbian. For as long as I could remember I wanted nothing to do with anything that my parents saw as girly, and boys always left me cold. When my girlfriends were arguing over which boy band member or vampire or werewolf was sexier or cuter, I didn't have any opinion because I was drawn to Kate Winslet and Britney Spears and Jennifer Lopez. I'd never had a real boyfriend, all the way through high school, and all I could think about was getting away from that dying and oppressive Midwestern town I grew up in. I played volleyball and softball, but had to be a cheerleader to appease my mother's desire for me to be a normal girl. I didn't like to wear dresses or skirts but I did have a sense of fashion. As soon as I had unsupervised access to the internet I started researching lesbians, and lesbian culture. My parents didn't want me to go to design school in New York, but I got a full scholarship and they agreed to help me with some of the expenses. I tried not to ever go back to that wretched little town. The last time I spoke to my mother she told me I was dead to her until I decided to live my life in a Christian manner. The last words I said to my mother were *Go to hell* as I disconnected the call.

Yes, Charlotte, I'd given up my family so I could live my life honestly, but I would jump into bed with the first good-looking straight guy that showed an interest in me—my wife's brother, no less, to maximize the damage caused, I guess.

"How very dare you." I wiped the tears away. "And that you think so little of me that even if that were humanly possible, that I would go for your brother? I mean, what kind of horrible person do you think I am, Charlotte? That's why I ran away. Not because of any feelings I had for Bast, but because the person I loved more than anything in the world thought I was such a terrible person, that I was somehow capable of doing something so disgusting. Do you really think that, Charlotte? Is that what you think of me?"

"I'm sorry," she said softly. "I was wrong. But you have to understand how it looked, and after Lindsay—"

"I'm not Lindsay, I'm nothing like Lindsay." I kept my head turned away from her. "And Bast—I thought Bast was my friend. I was bored and lonely because you worked all the time and when you weren't working you were tired. I'm at fault here, too, Charlotte. I shouldn't have blamed you for my boredom and gotten angry with you and frustrated. I should have gone back to work back then, back to Hollis. Maybe that would have helped, I don't know. But you really hurt me, thinking I would sleep with a man, let alone your brother. That made me feel like…if that was what you thought I was like, who I was, what chance did we have? I felt like there wasn't even anything left to fight for at that point, and you never even tried." My voice broke. "You didn't even try to talk to me, didn't come after me. You have no idea how bad I wanted you to, Charlotte. So many times I wanted to call you, come to your office, come out to Sea Oats, say I was sorry—but you made it clear you wanted nothing to do with me. I couldn't blame you. I mean, if you thought I would do something like that…well, I wouldn't want anything to do with me, either."

She reached over and took my hand. "I'm sorry, Ariel. I am. I've been sorry ever since I came home from work and found you were gone." Her voice broke. "I—I thought you'd come back, you know? I didn't think you were gone for good. It never even crossed my mind you wouldn't come back, that we wouldn't be able to work things out somehow. I kept hoping. Even after you got the apartment in the city and went back to work, I kept thinking you'd come back, and kept thinking, because I wanted to believe it, that you didn't come back because I was right. I've been so miserable, Ariel, so lost and lonely. And the other day, when I saw you there by the maze, I was so excited to see you—"

"You didn't act like it."

She laughed. "This is literally the worst time you could have come back, Ariel. With everything that's going on with the company, that was all I meant, that I couldn't give you the attention you deserved. Until we beat back this takeover bid, I have to give that my full attention. But once that's over, and all this mess with Angus being killed, I want us to sit down and figure this out, Ariel. I've never stopped loving you."

"What about Lindsay?"

"Lindsay?" She was clearly startled, not sure what I meant. "I'm not interested in Lindsay."

"Haven't you had a couple of dates?"

She laughed. "I've had dinner with her a couple of times, Ariel. That's all. And it was two friends who've known each other a long time having dinner, nothing more than that. Lindsay and I have been over for a long time. She has control of a small block of Swann's stock, and I need to make sure that she votes with the family. Are you still jealous of her? You never had a reason to be, you know. I've not felt that way about Lindsay for years before I even met you."

"Well, I wasn't exactly the most mature person in the world back then." I sighed. "I should have talked to you, we could have figured out how to make things work. You didn't ask me to give up my career, *I* did that on my own." If I was going to be honest...might as well go all the way. "The truth is, I was bored. If I'd just kept working, kept myself busy..."

"No." She took my hand in hers. "You shouldn't blame yourself. It was just as much my fault as it was yours." She kissed my cheek. "I spend too much time focused on my work. I always have. I didn't make enough time for you, didn't listen to you—I mean, clearly my friendship with Lindsay bothered you. And she *was* a bitch to you." She gave my hand a quick squeeze and let it go. "I just thought it was all something that would blow over. I loved you, and cared about Lindsay"— she raised her hand to stop me from responding—"as a friend, and thought you two would become friends on your own. You have a lot in common."

"Besides you?"

She smiled faintly. "Besides me. But I should have realized how it made you feel, and taken you more seriously. That's on me. The last two years without you have been so lonely, so empty. You have no idea how many times I wanted to call you, wanted to stop by your office or your apartment, but you were doing so well with your career…"

"I love what I do, Charlotte, but I also love you." There. I'd said it.

"When I heard you scream, and saw you hanging there"— she went on like I hadn't said anything—"all I could think about was how awful life would be if you weren't around. I've been a fool. I shouldn't have let things go on this way for so long."

"We were both fools." I took her hand again. "God, I'm afraid I'm going to open my eyes and this whole thing will turn out to have been a dream."

"Are you saying what I think you're saying?" She put our linked hands on my knee.

"I can always blame it on hitting my head later," I joked. "But yes, I do still love you, Charlotte. I'd like for us to figure out a way to make this work. I don't want a divorce. I want us to work this all out. I'm not giving up my job, and I won't be an idiot like I was again, okay?"

She pulled in to the parking lot of the hospital and parked in the first open slot. She turned off the engine and leaned over the console and kissed me.

I kissed her back and put my arms around her. The tears I'd been holding back began falling down my cheeks. Even though every muscle in my body ached, despite the dull throb in my head, my heart was swelling with joy.

I hadn't dared dream this would be possible.

And yet it was. She loved me, she really loved me, and we were going to make it through everything.

"Let's get you inside and checked out," she whispered, pulling back from me and smiling. "So we can get you back home. And I'm never letting you go again, do you understand me?"

CHAPTER TWELVE

Charlotte stayed with me the whole time, holding my hand. It seemed like we were at the hospital forever—my cuts and abrasions being treated and bandaged, my entire body being x-rayed before being pronounced okay. I balked at going to another hospital for a CAT scan to see if I had a concussion, but agreed to come back if I started vomiting or having dizzy spells.

The sun was coming up when we finally walked out of the emergency room doors, hand in hand, on our way to her car.

She hugged and kissed me before unlocking the doors. "I'm sorry this happened to you," she said, "but if this was what it took to get us back together..."

"Hopefully the next time we have a fight I won't have to almost die to patch things up," I replied.

"You're sure you want to do this?" she asked.

"Yes."

She'd tried to explain to me in simple terms what was going on with Swann's between my X-rays and other tests, pausing whenever a nurse or a doctor came by to check on me or do another test.

Before we'd met, there had been a bit of crisis with the company's finances. Swann's was still going strong, but surviving the last economic downturn had left the company with very little operational cash. There was also an opportunity for Swann's to expand into the Eastern European market, to take over another department store chain that was about to shut its doors, but there wasn't any cash to buy the other chain. After consulting with Roger and the lawyers, Charlotte decided the best way to handle the expansion was to take the company public. She was able to get the trust dissolved relatively quickly—she only needed Bast's agreement—but she and Bast maintained enough shares in Swann's to keep an unshakable majority in the company, and therefore control. The stock sale had gone better than they ever could have imagined, and everything was fine.

"Until I was alerted that a dummy corporation was buying up shares of Swann's last year," she said grimly. "At the time, this was just an annoyance. I felt that Swann's was safe—even if someone bought up all the outstanding shares, they wouldn't be able to take control. In retrospect, I should have liquidated some assets and tried to buy back as much of the stock as I could. But I thought I could count on Bast."

Always a mistake, I thought, but didn't say out loud. I was going to have to figure out how to be around Bast—he was family, no matter what had happened in the past. If Charlotte and I were going to work out, I was going to have to work things out with Bast, too.

Hopefully, Kayla would be sticking around for a while. I had a feeling she'd be good for him.

"And me," I said instead.

She gave me a look. "What do you mean?"

I laughed at her expression. "We didn't sign a prenup. If I divorced you…" I laughed even harder when I realized that had never occurred to her. That was also reassuring. She wasn't trying to use me to protect her stock.

"Oh my God." She moaned. "You didn't think—"

"It did cross my mind once I found out about the stock mess," I admitted. "Well, keep that in mind the next time we disagree about something—I could end up with half your stock."

"I'll give it to you, if you want it," she said, kissing my hand. "I'd give you anything to make you happy, to make sure you never leave my side again."

"Yeah, well, the stock is pretty good leverage," I joked.

"I'll keep that in mind, believe me. Anyway, Bast had this great opportunity to invest in a dating app"—she made a sour face—"whatever that means."

I laughed. Charlotte's smartphone was wasted on her. She wouldn't know or care what an app was.

She frowned at me. "Well, I read the prospectus and told him he was crazy to invest in it, and I also refused to release money from the trust for him to use toward it. It never occurred to me that he would borrow against his Swann's stock to get the money he needed." She shook her head. "And of course, the app didn't quite turn out right and he lost all the money and is defaulting on the loan. I've been making the payments for him, but I don't know how long I can keep it up."

"Can't you both just release the money from the trust to pay for it?"

"There isn't enough money in the trust to cover how much he lost." Her face was grim. "Yeah, it's that bad. I don't know what he was thinking. This isn't one of his little scrapes where Peggy or I can write a check and make it all better. He could lose his stock, and if he does, we'll lose control of the company. I am very close to finding out who is behind this takeover attempt. Lindsay is actually helping me, but we just haven't been able to get to the bottom of it."

Typical Lindsay, I thought, *what could she possibly do to help?* But anything to get closer to Charlotte.

"And I'm running out of time," she went on. "I don't know, maybe I should just sell my stock and stop fighting, retire and let Swann's go. But I'm afraid that new management would just strip the business and sell off its assets and close it down. And I can't let that happen. I can't just let Swann's go down the drain."

"Do you think whoever killed Angus has something to do with this?"

"I don't know how." She shook her head. "Angus wasn't involved with anything other than the grounds, and the maze mostly. I can't make sense of his death."

Whoever had tried to throw me off the roof was probably the same person who'd killed Angus and thought I was a witness or might figure out who it was—even though my pictures were basically useless. But why kill Angus? It didn't make any sense.

The truth's at the center of the maze, Miss Ariel, remember that—at the center of the maze.

But what did the maze have to do with anything?

I yawned as she started the car and revved the engine. I fell asleep as we drove out of the parking lot and didn't wake up again until she stopped at the foot of the stairs. I got out into the chill of the morning, the grass wet with dew, but at least the clouds were clearing and we were finally going to have a sunny day. I waited for her to park the car and we went up the stairs together. She helped me up the stairs, and hesitated when we got to the flight to the third floor. "You could move back into our old room," she said hesitatingly.

I kissed her on the cheek. "As much as I would like that, let's slow down a bit," I replied. "It makes me really happy that you want me to, though."

She smiled back at me. "Okay, let's get you upstairs." She helped me into bed, and as I laid my head back against my pillows, she asked me if I felt okay. They'd given me painkillers at the hospital and so nothing hurt anymore.

"Good."

"I'll have someone get your prescription filled as soon as the CVS in town opens this morning," she said from the door. I heard the click as she locked it, and then the door shut behind her.

I woke to bright sunshine and hurting everywhere a few hours later. I sat up in the bed—it was just after ten—and there was a brown prescription bottle sitting on my nightstand that hadn't been there the night before. It was my pain pills, and as I shook one out I wondered how they'd gotten into my room, since Charlotte had locked the door when she left. *Peggy must have keys*, I realized as I ran the tap to get some cold water in the bathroom. *Of course she does. So locking the door is pointless.* My head still ached, and once I took the pill and emptied the water glass, I stared at myself in the mirror. My hair looked horrific, my eyes were bloodshot, and the bags under my eyes were enormous, purple and bruised looking. My arms were covered in bandages, and my fingers were throbbing from hanging on to the side of the roof. My palms were scratched up, painted orange with antiseptic over the scrapes and gouges.

Gingerly and carefully I washed my face and brushed my teeth, then put on a pair of jeans and an NYU sweatshirt before heading down the back stairs in search of some much needed coffee.

Maeve was in the kitchen, and Kayla was sitting at the kitchen table staring off into space like a zombie. I helped myself to some coffee, as Maeve clucked and hovered over me, trying to make sure I was okay and babying me, which I gently refused. I sat down next to Kayla, who blinked at me a couple of times before her eyes seemed to focus and she saw me.

"I haven't slept," she mumbled, barely audibly. "I couldn't fall back asleep after you went to the hospital and I was afraid to take another pill and so I'm drinking coffee to try to stay awake so I can sleep tonight." She gave me a sheepish smile, as Maeve grunted derisively. "I wanted to talk to you. Can we go back up to your room and talk?"

"Sure. Maeve, would you mind bringing up a breakfast tray?" Maeve nodded, and I followed Kayla back up the stairs to my room.

Even without sleep, even though she wasn't my type, I had to admit she was stunningly beautiful. Loose strands of hair floated around her face, and her skin, even without makeup, glowed like it was lit from within, like one of the movie stars from the old black-and-white days.

She yawned sleepily.

"You're not going to make it till tonight," I said.

She shrugged, her slender shoulders barely moving. "I'm trying to get on a better sleep schedule," she said with another yawn. "Once Bast and me are married, we're not going to be doing the nightlife thing anymore. I want to have kids."

The thought of Bast as a father was terrifying. "Has he asked you?"

She shook her head. "Not yet, but I know he will. He loves me."

I felt bad for her. How many women had Bast gone through during my year at Sea Oats? Too many to count. Much as I liked Kayla, I didn't see Bast settling down with any woman, not just her. But it wasn't my place to tell her, was it?

But stranger things have happened. Maybe this mess with

the stock was just the thing to make Bast get his act together and settle down.

"What did you want to talk to me about?" I asked, just as Maeve knocked on the door and brought in the breakfast tray. She set it down and closed the door behind her. I poured us each a cup of coffee.

"I wasn't completely truthful last night—this morning—when I said I didn't wake up until you screamed." She yawned. "I took a sleeping pill but I couldn't sleep. I was awake."

"Wasn't Bast with you?"

She giggled. "You know Peggy doesn't let Bast and me share a room—she's kind of old-fashioned about that sort of thing, and besides, I always have trouble sleeping." She made a sour face. "I don't want to keep him up, so…" She shrugged again. "So he went downstairs to his room to go to sleep after we, you know"—she winked—"and I took a shower and took a pill and turned the television on and I heard something out in the hall. I opened my door and I looked out and I saw someone go up the attic stairs."

I blinked at her a few times. "Wait, you mean to say you saw who it was? You're going to have to tell the police! Who was it?"

"I don't want to talk to the police, do I have to?" She pouted. She really was just a child. "And I didn't really see who it was, you know? I just saw someone go through the doorway from behind. It was a man," she amended, "and he was wearing jeans and a dark long coat, and he had a hat on, so I couldn't recognize him, and I don't know if I would know him again. I just thought you should know." She took a drink of her coffee and smiled at me. "You should know someone is trying to kill you." She put her hand up to the side of her face. "You've got to be careful, Ariel. These people here aren't what they seem."

"That's an understatement," I replied with a slight smile.

"You can't trust anyone here," she whispered, leaning closer to me. "Not even me. No one here can be trusted."

She was falling asleep, so I got her up and helped her as much as I could to her room, and she was asleep before her head hit the pillow. I limped back to my room and slipped back into bed. The pain pill was making me groggy. I ate the breakfast and put the tray down on the floor, getting back under the covers and lying down. My aches and pains began to slowly leave my body, and it felt like I was becoming one with the bed, which was kind of lovely and nice. I was vaguely aware of calling out when someone knocked on the door, and then Peggy let herself in with a key.

You can't trust anyone here.

The truth's in the center of the maze.

None of it made sense.

Peggy smiled at me, and stroked my forehead gently. "*Shhhhhh,*" she said as I tried to talk, and I didn't know what was wrong with me. Everything was fading in and out of focus. This was more than the pain pill making me loopy and I wondered about Kayla and her falling asleep so quickly and easily, when she claimed she had insomnia and I remembered the tray Maeve had brought up and maybe…maybe there was something in the coffee?

Peggy and Maeve have access to all the keys.

One of them could have searched my room, easily.

Kayla—Kayla hadn't been sure who it was who'd gone up to the roof. She'd just seen a hat and jeans and a long coat. It could have been a woman.

It could have been Peggy.

Could Peggy be the one who was behind everything?

She was humming to herself as she arranged the covers around me, and she gave me a little smile when she noticed me looking at her. "You shouldn't have come back, Ariel," she said softly. "You're not safe here at Sea Oats, you know."

I could feel my mind starting to go, starting to wander off. What had she given me? And Kayla?

Peggy would do anything for Bast.

I needed to get away from her. I needed to get away from here.

I tried to talk but my mouth didn't seem to want to work.

Peggy kissed my forehead and went back out of the room.

I forced myself to sit up in the bed. My head felt like it weighed a hundred pounds.

The coffee.

Had she drugged me and Kayla both? I somehow managed to pour out another cup. Maybe it was the pain pill, maybe it was the combination of being hurt and sore and not sleeping much and taking a pain pill, maybe I was making the whole thing up in my tired mind. Peggy wouldn't hurt me, she wouldn't do anything to hurt Charlotte, even to help Bast she wouldn't chose between the two of them that way, would she, she never had before.

I sniffed the coffee and it smelled like coffee, it tasted like coffee, so I took another drink and finished the cup and poured out another as I continued to get loopier.

Peggy wouldn't have drugged me, she wouldn't—

When I woke up it was dark.

I sat up in bed, sore and tired and thirsty. Thunder roared outside as I reached for the lamp on the nightstand and switched it on. It was after six—I'd slept the whole day away and it was pitch black outside and I could tell it was going to rain any moment.

The breakfast tray was gone.

I put on my shoes.

Someone in the house was trying to kill me.

But why, Peggy? Why me?

I needed to get out of the house.

I grabbed my jacket and pulled it around me. I crept down the back stairs and ran into Bast coming out of the kitchen. He grabbed at me and I pulled away.

"Hey, I need to talk to you!"

"Stay away from me!" I shouted at him, holding up my hands to ward him off.

Bast. And Peggy. It had to be.

Bast was the only person Peggy would do anything criminal for. It made sense.

He grabbed hold of me but I pulled away from him. "I said stay away from me!"

"Ariel, please, you don't understand—"

I pulled away from him and went out the back door and down the back stairs. I heard the back door slam—he was coming behind me. I ran, slipping and sliding on the wet pavement as the thunder roared overhead and lightning lit up the sky. It was dark, very dark, and it was going to pour and I didn't know where I was going but I needed to get away. Bast was calling after me. I looked back over my shoulder and saw he was carrying a gun.

"Ariel! Ariel!" I could hear him calling but all I could think about was the gun in his hand.

A gun.

He had a gun.

And he was coming after me.

Terror gave me a rush of adrenaline and I ran the wrong way, thinking crazily I would duck around the maze and head for the road on the other side. Why Bast wanted to kill me, why Peggy was helping him, I didn't know—

"Ariel!"

It was Roger, and he was standing in the entrance to the

maze. He beckoned to me, and I ran over to the maze and, panting, ducked inside.

"Go inside," he whispered to me. "You'll be safe from him inside."

My legs turned to water as I looked at the hedge towering above me on every side.

"Ariel!" Bast was calling me still, and Roger pushed me behind him.

And pulled a gun of his own out of his pocket.

I was such a fool.

It all made sense, finally.

Roger. It had been Roger all along.

Roger, who had helped engineer the sale of Swann's stock when the company went public.

Roger, who'd asked Peggy to marry him.

It had been Roger I'd seen out there on the lawn with Lindsay. Lindsay wanted to see the pictures to see if she could recognize Roger.

"Why, Roger?" I asked. "I thought you were my friend."

He smiled at me, and shoved the gun into my side. "You know who my mother was, Ariel? Her last name was Malone."

Malone. The Malone Group, Brigid Malone.

"You hate them as much as I do, don't you, Ariel?" he whispered. "Bast ruined your life, didn't he? I'll just shoot him, and you'll play along, won't you? Everyone will believe he wanted to kill you, won't they?"

I could hear the madness in his voice, see the way his eyes glittered. He'd hated the Swanns for years, wanted vengeance on the family because of the way his ancestress had been treated...But he was just as much a Swann as the rest of them.

He hated them so much. He wanted to take the company away from them, Peggy away from Charlotte and Bast.

And me. He wanted to take me away from Charlotte.

He wanted them to suffer. That was why he'd lured me to the roof.

"Bast! He has a gun!" I shoved Roger as hard as I could and his gun went off as he crashed into the side of the hedge. I couldn't get past him, so I gritted my teeth and closed my eyes and ran deeper into the maze.

I went around a corner and it was dark, too dark to see. I heard another gunshot and hoped Bast was all right as I felt my way along inside the hedge maze. I'd never been more terrified in my life.

The only time I'd ever been in the hedge before was when, ironically, Bast had dared me to face my fears and go inside to find my way around. The maze wasn't difficult to solve, but there were a lot of wrong turns and dead ends, and it was cropped so close to the ground you couldn't escape from underneath it. I'd gotten lost, of course, unable to find my way out, and had lost control, screaming and crying, and then old Angus had appeared out of nowhere, taken my hand, and led me to the center of the maze.

"Always remember, Miss Ariel, that if you get lost in the maze you just come to the center," he'd said, pointing at the ground. On the ground was a design of the maze with an arrow showing the quickest way out. "Just find the center and you can always find your way out."

The truth's in the center of the maze.

And then I remembered, and I knew what Angus had been trying so hard to tell me, to warn me about.

Roger was the one who'd put the key there in the center, after a child had gotten lost in the maze and she'd panicked and there were worries about insurance liabilities. Roger had suggested that a map be put in the direct center, so anyone who got lost just had to come to the center and find their way back out again.

Angus was telling me it was Roger, that Roger was the one I had to beware of, who was out to ruin the family.

Roger, who'd engineered the breaking of the trust and the sale of stock.

Roger, engaged now to Peggy, who could have easily drugged the coffee Peggy had brought me and Kayla.

I groped my way along as it started to rain, the cold wetness saturating my clothes quickly, wishing I'd brought my phone with me. I heard another gunshot, frighteningly close, and tried to rein in my emotions, tried to not lose my head. I just had to find the center and I could find my way out.

If Roger wasn't waiting for me there.

"Ariel!" I heard Charlotte calling over the sound of the storm as I went around another corner, and there before me was a dark form facing the other way.

Lightning flashed and I saw it was Roger.

Charlotte was at the end of the row.

He was aiming at her.

I jumped on him, knocking his arm up, and the gun went off again as we both went down in a tangle of arms and legs and he slapped me hard and I clawed at his face and we rolled over into the hedge, the branches clawing at my arms and my hands and my face, and he was on top of me and he was putting his hands around my throat and I couldn't breathe and my ears were ringing and I heard another gunshot.

And the pressure on my throat went slack.

Sobbing, I shoved him off me and scrabbled to my feet just as sunlight broke through the clouds again.

Bast was standing there, holding a gun, and Charlotte rushed over to me, taking me in her arms. "Are you all right?"

I nodded. "I think so."

"You saved my life," Bast said.

"And mine," Charlotte added.

I just nodded. "Is he…?"

Bast knelt down beside him. "Yes, he's dead."

"Poor Peggy." I buried my face in Charlotte's shoulder.

"Better she finds out now than after she married him," Charlotte said grimly. "I suspected Roger was behind the stock takeover, but this…"

"Angus must have seen him break into your office and confronted him"—I shook my head—"and got killed for his trouble. And he thought I had pictures of him with Angus, so I had to be killed, too."

"Let's get into the house and call the police," Charlotte put her arm around me. "Come on, Bast."

And we headed back up the walk to the house, and to our future.

I would never walk out on Charlotte again.

About the Author

Valerie Bronwen is a retired journalist and former writing instructor from New Orleans. Her first published short story, "The Other Side of the Mirror," appeared in the anthology *Women of the Dark Streets*. Valerie is a long-time fan of the mystery genre. Her first novel, *Slash and Burn*, was a Lambda Literary Award finalist, and she is working on her third novel in her home on Coliseum Square in New Orleans.

Books Available From Bold Strokes Books

A Lamentation of Swans by Valerie Bronwen. Ariel Montgomery returns to Sea Oats to try to save her broken marriage but soon finds herself also fighting to save her own life and catch a murderer. (978-1-62639-828-3)

Freedom to Love by Ronica Black. What happens when the woman who spent her life worrying about caring for her family finally finds the freedom to love without borders? (978-1-63555-001-6)

House of Fate by Barbara Ann Wright. Two women must throw off the lives they've known as a guardian and an assassin and save two rival houses before their secrets tear the galaxy apart. (978-1-62639-780-4)

Planning for Love by Erin Dutton. Could true love be the one thing that wedding coordinator Faith McKenna didn't plan for? (978-1-62639-954-9)

Sidebar by Carsen Taite. Judge Camille Avery and her clerk, attorney West Fallon, agree on little except their mutual attraction, but can their relationship and their careers survive a headline-grabbing case? (978-1-62639-752-1)

Sweet Boy and Wild One by T. L. Hayes. When Rachel Cole meets soulful singer Bobby Layton at an open mic, she is immediately in thrall. What she soon discovers will rock her world in ways she never imagined. (978-1-62639-963-1)

To Be Determined by Mardi Alexander and Laurie Eichler. Charlie Dickerson escapes her life in the US to rescue Australian wildlife with Pip Atkins, but can they save each other? (978-1-62639-946-4)

True Colors by Yolanda Wallace. Blogger Robby Rawlins plans to use First Daughter Taylor Crenshaw to get ahead, but she never planned on falling in love with her in the process. (978-1-62639-927-3)

Heart Stop by Radclyffe. Two women, one with a damaged body, the other a damaged spirit, challenge each other to dare to live again. (978-1-62639-899-3)

Undercover Affairs by Julie Blair. Searching for stolen documents crucial to U.S. security, CIA agent Rett Spenser confronts lies, deceit, and unexpected romance as she investigates art gallery owner Shannon Kent. (978-1-62639-905-1)

Unexpected by Jenny Frame. When Dale McGuire falls for Rebecca Harper, the mother of the son she never knew she had, will Rebecca's troubled past stop them from making the family they both truly crave? (978-1-62639-942-6)

Canvas for Love by Charlotte Greene. When ghosts from Amelia's past threaten to undermine their relationship, Chloé must navigate the greatest romance of her life without losing sight of who she is. (978-1-62639-944-0)

Repercussions by Jessica L. Webb. Someone planted information in Edie Black's brain and now they want it back, but with the protection of shy former soldier Skye Kenny, Edie has a chance at life and love. (978-1-62639-925-9)

Spark by Catherine Friend. Jamie's life is turned upside down when her consciousness travels back to 1560 and lands in the body of one of Queen Elizabeth I's ladies-in-waiting...or has she totally lost her grip on reality? (978-1-62639-930-3)

Taking Sides by Kathleen Knowles. When passion and politics collide, can love survive? (978-1-62639-876-4)

Thorns of the Past by Gun Brooke. Former cop Darcy Flynn's heart broke when her career on the force ended in disgrace, but perhaps saving Sabrina Hawk's life will mend it in more ways than one. (978-1-62639-857-3)

You Make Me Tremble by Karis Walsh. Seismologist Casey Radnor comes to the San Juan Islands to study an earthquake but finds her heart shaken by passion when she meets animal rescuer Iris Mallery. (978-1-62639-901-3)

Girls Next Door, edited by Sandy Lowe and Stacia Seaman. Best-selling romance authors tell it from the heart—sexy, romantic stories of falling for the girls next door. (978-1-62639-916-7)

Complications by MJ Williamz. Two women battle for the heart of one. (978-1-62639-769-9)

Crossing the Wide Forever by Missouri Vaun. As Cody Walsh and Lillie Ellis face the perils of the untamed West, they discover that love's uncharted frontier isn't for the weak in spirit or the faint of heart. (978-1-62639-851-1)

Fake It till You Make It by M. Ullrich. Lies will lead to trouble, but can they lead to love? (978-1-62639-923-5)

Pursuit by Jackie D. The pursuit of the most dangerous terrorist in America will crack the lines of friendship and love, and not everyone will make it out from under the weight of duty and service. (978-1-62639-903-7)

The Practitioner by Ronica Black. Sometimes love comes calling whether you're ready for it or not. (978-1-62639-948-8)

Unlikely Match by Fiona Riley. When an ambitious PR exec and her super-rich coding geek-girl client fall in love, they learn that giving something up may be the only way to have everything. (978-1-62639-891-7)

Where Love Leads by Erin McKenzie. A high school counselor and the mom of her new student bond in support of the troubled girl, never expecting deeper feelings to emerge, testing the boundaries of their relationship. (978-1-62639-991-4)

Forsaken Trust by Meredith Doench. When four women are murdered, Agent Luce Hansen must regain trust in her most valuable investigative tool—herself—to catch the killer. (978-1-62639-737-8)

Letter of the Law by Carsen Taite. Will federal prosecutor Bianca Cruz take a chance at love with horse breeder Jade Vargas, whose dark family ties threaten everything Bianca has worked to protect—including her child? (978-1-62639-750-7)

New Life by Jan Gayle. Trigena and Karrie are having a baby, but the stress of becoming a mother and the impact on their relationship might be too much for Trigena. (978-1-62639-878-8)